Wolf's Path

Wolf's Path

JOYCE CHNG

Atthis Arts

Wolf's Path

Published by Atthis Arts, LLC
Detroit, Michigan
atthisarts.com

ISBN 978-1-961654-32-7

Library of Congress Control Number: 2025930442

This body is
soft loam
a forest
a soaring murmuration
weaving

down to
earth

a mech thromping down
an enemy robot
cyborg steel

spreading wings
phoenix like

desiring flight
a huge galaxy
swirling nebula
binary planets twinning

transforming
shift

within a running wolf
four-pawed, howling.

Introduction

They say a wolf learns about its land over the years by sniffing, exploring and crossing borders. The wolf builds its own external (and internal) landscape which becomes a map of places the wolf can hunt, walk without fear, and explore further.

I often equate my walking path to that of the wolf's. At times, uncertain and anxious. At other times, exuberant and I want to howl for joy. In between there are the moments of defeat and immense sadness, of lost opportunities and failed hunts. But across the span of seventeen years, I have built my own landscape and will continue to do so.

The collection is arranged in three sections: New Trails, Terrain, and The Land. New Trails, as the words say, contains stories when I was starting out as a writer. It was 2007. I had resigned from teaching, the outlook felt bleak, and I was lost. I turned to the thing I knew how to do best: writing. 2009 was the year I started submitting for real, to semipro venues. I was also pregnant with my youngest. Once more, it felt like destination unknown. Terrain holds the stories written when I was still finding my footing, gaining my confidence and combating impostor syndrome. I was finding my voice, so to speak, to howl. Around this time, I was also dealing with a breast disease that almost destroyed my immune system and gave me chronic fatigue. I just wrote on, beset by inexplicable exhaustion. Lastly, The Land sees its fruition with a selection of more recent stories published during the pandemic. This is the phase I am at now: I know my land, I have my own map, and I know how to navigate the terrain. Readers might have their own ideas of common themes and motifs in my stories . . . But these are the stories that represent the various stages of my writing path.

Most of the stories have been published previously in some form, in anthologies or at venues. One might say I am repeating myself. I say why not? I will howl until I hear the answering howl from people like me.

New Trails

A Matter Of Possession

Admiral Wu sat in the executive office sumptuously appointed in a personal favorite style—a lot of calligraphy and embroidery framed in lacquered rosewood. There was the mild fragrance of jasmine tea in the air, the sound of waves and the soft *tick-tock* of the clock with the golden mechanical canary on the mantle. Exquisitely painted portraits of family members and her child graced the large table. It was an idyllic moment and savored immensely like fine mellowed Burgundy wine, another personal favorite. Of course, the moment would not be complete without the ornately carved teak betel box, filled with areca nuts and betel leaves to be chewed. An acquired taste, of course, from a tour of duty in the seas of Java; the other officers had found the taste strange and unfavorable.

It was indeed a rare moment. Paperwork had to be done with many files requiring her official acknowledgement. This was done with the usual red seal, carved with rank, name and ship's name. Reports had to be written; at the moment, the stenograph was being prepared by Ensign Han Xing, a young lad eager to please his commanding officer. He was outside the office, waiting to be called in.

Oh, just a few minutes longer for tea. Yet, such thinking was indulgent. There were duties to be done, tasks to be accomplished. The Imperial vessel *Feng Huang* was not an idle ship.

A fastidious check of uniform, adorned with a braid corded with golden thread and a marker of seniority, very much in the style of the Western nations. There was another set of uniform, courtlier in fashion with brocaded sleeves and pants, in the executive cabin.

It was time. The tea had already been drunk and enjoyed in private. The poor ensign was perhaps impatient now. The bell was pressed and within a few seconds, Ensign Han Xing's earnest face appeared at the door. He was twenty, having passed his Imperial Academy examinations two years ago. He had proven himself to be reliable, though a little pompous at times. He bore the stenograph, embossed of course with dragons and phoenixes, very carefully. It was a work of art, a gift from her family when the promotion to admiral was announced a year ago.

"Yes, Admiral Wu?" He snapped to attention; the stenograph held in front of him stiffly.

"Please. Come in."

Ensign Han Xing went obediently to the side of the large mahogany table, his usual place, when he worked the stenograph. He set up the apparatus and waited expectantly, his ruddy face alert, eyes bright.

"How are the cadets settling in?" Admiral Wu asked softly. The eight cadets were fresh from the Imperial Academy, sent to her ship for practical attachment. She took special interest in the eight, because they were all girls, scions from a number of aristocratic and merchant families. A long time ago, she was like them, in a pioneer batch for 'fair maidens' to join the illustrious Imperial Academy.

Ensign Han Xing answered, his tone neutral, just as he was taught: "They have settled down, my lord. They find their accommodations to their satisfaction. Cadets Xiao and Lee are experiencing slight discomfort and are coping at the moment."

Admiral Wu had to stifle a smile. The constant rolling and pitching of the ship was something that the cadets had to get used too. They had to be prepared, eventually, for lift-off too, because the *Feng Huang*, like all the *Hai Feng*-class ships, had aero capabilities. Training at the Imperial Academy was one thing. Being on an actual ship was another. She remembered how her stomach lurched when the ship she apprenticed on—the *Peony*—went into emergency evasive maneuvers in mid-air, to avoid collision with the *Mountain Spirit* which was approaching too rapidly. The helmsman of the *Peony* was reprimanded by the then commanding officer for his negligence.

All officers of Her Imperial Majesty's Aero-Nautical Navy had to be impeccable in their duties, honorable and steadfast in what they did. Negligence was a blemish in personal records. She knew that it was not entirely the helmsman's fault; she recalled his name was Xu. But he bore the brunt of the commanding officer's wrath. She hoped that the eight cadets would become good officers. They had after all gone through the rigorous basic training and had proven that they were physically and mentally fit. *And young,* she thought ruefully. *With youthful idealism still in their eyes and hearts.* It would be a steep learning curve for them.

The *Feng Huang* swayed a little. The sea was a little rough today. The stability was soon adjusted by the ship's inbuilt ballast and Wu decided that she would look into the reports now. She signaled Han Xing who sat up straighter, fingers poised on the keyboard. Time to be impeccable in her duties now.

Morning brought fog and a bone-chilling cold. Most of the sailors and supervising officers wore their standard-issue wool-lined cloaks marked with the emblem of the Imperial Armed Forces: a golden stylized dragon. The *Feng Huang* creaked and responded to the cold weather. Already the boilers in the engine room were working hard to provide steam as well as warmth for the cabins.

Commander Tsang found herself blowing on her fingers while she was overseeing training. The ensigns and the cadets were going through the routine calisthenics, timed with rhythmic drumbeats. She was pleased that the eight girls—*they looked so young!*—were keeping up with their male counterparts. At least their feet were not bound, and they were not in flimsy silks. They were doing something productive and the Navy certainly needed their contributions. She had already heard rumors that the commanding brass might launch an all-female ship. But rumors were rumors; if the interfering lazy eunuchs had their way, there would not be any female officer in the Navy.

Cadets Xiao and Lee were looking better now, after their bout of motion sickness. They would cope, in due time. Ming, Tang, Chu, and Wang were going through their self-defense punches with some gusto. The two quieter ones, Ling and Ouyang, were diligent enough.

Suddenly something fell from the sky, a bright star-like object blazing a trail across the heavens. It arced, as if Hou Yi the divine archer was practicing his shots, high and wide. A splash and an explosion followed when it impacted. It was loud enough to make the *Feng Huang* shiver in response.

The calisthenics halted abruptly, with the ensigns and cadets gaping at the phenomenon.

"Stay in focus," Tsang rapped out sharply, even though her curiosity was piqued. The youngsters scrambled into action again, afraid to earn her wrath. A movement drew her attention to the helm. Admiral Wu had emerged from her office, wrapped in her cloak. She too had seen the strange star fall.

﷼

"Do you know what that phenomenon actually is?"

The ship was speeding full steam ahead in the direction of the impact, the wind harsh against exposed facial skin. The two senior officers stood at the helm manned by Navigator Deng.

"A meteorite, perhaps?" Wu turned to face her first officer. "It was uncommonly bright."

They had just received urgent code from the brass to retrieve the stellar object so that the Imperial scientists could start their investigations. A meteorite could provide so much information about the solar system as well as other essential questions like military defense and protection. So, the Imperial vessel *Feng Huang* was rushing to the scene as fast as her boilers could manage. Imagine how the discovery would galvanize research—and Imperial China would leap forward with technological advancements.

"My lord, we are approaching the target," Navigator Deng announced respectfully, and the ship slowed discernibly from full steam to gentle cruise. There were sea gulls riding the wind, their wings white against grey, dipping in and out of the fog like spirits. They were circling above something in the water, squawking away in a chaotic chorus.

Commander Tsang peered into the churning sea, amused that some sea birds were floating on the surface of the water. She peered more closely and spied something dark, like coffee, half-submerged in water. It was *huge,* as big as an Imperial carriage and surprising light as well, bobbing noticeably with the current. The *Feng Huang* drew up beside the object and the two women could see that the object was also obsidian in color, looking like some dark jewel. Floating. Was it porous? What kind of material was it made of? Where did it come from? Do rocks *float*?

"Not from the moon," Tsang hazarded a guess. "Chang'Er might be looking for a lost rock." Her wry humor made Wu smile a little. They were friends and had spent the Pioneer Years as roommates.

"It looks light," Wu leaned forward and made mental measurements of the size and weight. "I do not think it is an asteroid either. It looks … different." *Definitely for the stenograph,* she mused to herself. She made notes on the logistics of the imminent retrieval operation. Where was she going to *store* that huge thing? Would it contaminate the ship and her people with something nefarious?

A cry broke the silence. It was from the crow's nest. "Ship sighted!"

Tsang and Wu looked at each other. It was going to be *interesting.* No other Navy ship belonging to Imperial China was in the vicinity.

It was, as expected, not a familiar Navy ship making its way towards them. The make was different with a cumbersome-looking hull and ungainly body, clad in iron and smoking thick black smoke. A typical Western-style ironclad, as grey and grim as they came. Wu and Tsang had studied pictures and schematics of the ships belonging to the European West; they also encountered such ships in separate tours of duty. It looked like a British *Caesar*-class destroyer. Probably on border patrol and lucky enough to have spotted the bright star making its downward plunge.

For a moment, Wu thought of home, of the family courtyard pink with cherry blossoms in spring. Of children's laughter. Strange that in moments of potential anxious confrontations thoughts of home became important and precious. She turned to look at the dark object still floating on the water.

The ugly foreign vessel puffed its way up to a fair distance away from the *Feng Huang* but close enough to allow identification of vessel type and its size. As she guessed, Caesar-class and armed with visible gun-ports and turrets.

Wu breathed in deeply. She was trained in diplomacy; she astutely chose classes in diplomacy and relations with other foreign countries (and their navies). The British Empire was an ally of Imperial China, though some officials said it was an uneasy friendship fraught with intense rivalry and subtle jealousies. The relations with her British counterparts had been polite enough, though not as cordial as she would have expected. There were few women officers in their Navy staffed mostly by men. She steeled herself for a war, not only of words but also of pre-existing attitudes.

The foreign ship was already signaling, with colored flags. The commanding officer of that ship wanted to talk to her.

Tsang looked at her again. It was highly likely that the British vessel wanted the fallen star.

"Well met," Wu greeted the tall British officer with a warm enough tone and smiled, welcoming him into her executive room. The gentleman was dressed in a smart Naval uniform, almost similar to hers. Dark blue, with a red sash around his waist and a ceremonial saber at his side. The gentleman was around her age, late thirties and early forties. He was blonde, streaked with premature white. His blue eyes were examining her intently and she looked back at him unafraid. There were many foreign men who thought that Chinese women were dainty and docile, with a doll-like fragility. In terms of designation, she outranked him, and she was not some China doll, ornamental and pretty to look at. Her command of Queen's English was excellent, and she could read the man's expression: *disbelief.*

She had her dark hair pulled into a severe bun, pinned together with an ivory comb, having eschewed long hair for many years. Not when she was onboard her ship. It was highly inconvenient, especially when it came to hand-to-hand combat. Her skin was fair, though not like porcelain imagined by the European press. She was wearing leather boots, not embroidered silk slippers.

"Well met, madam," the gentleman said with a nod. "Let me introduce myself. I am Captain Richard Harper, of the Royal British Navy. My ship—" he indicated with a tilt of his chin, towards the porthole, "—is the HMS *Wolfhound.*"

"I am pleased to have made your acquaintance," Wu kept

her tone careful. *Cordial but careful.* It was obvious that Captain Richard Harper was also eyeing the floating stellar item.

"The *Wolfhound* was in the vicinity when we spotted a strange heavenly object," Harper started by saying, politely refusing the offer of jasmine tea. "We traced its impact to this particular area."

Wu inclined her head slightly. "So did we. My ship is on a retrieval mission."

Harper's nostrils flared a little. "We have received directions to recover the phenomenon as well."

There was a brief, electric moment of tension—the officers from two different navies sizing each other up. It reminded Wu of a dog-and-bone situation, with two dogs posturing over a tasty morsel. Her heart flamed brightly and waited for Harper to make his move. She watched him like an eagle watching a rabbit. He soon cleared his throat.

"May I suggest we share in the retrieval operation and take samples for our respective scientific investigations?" he said quietly and waited for *her* response. He was watching her just as she was watching him. Both wanted the whole object intact and she did not think that both of them were going to back away that easily.

"A good suggestion, sir," she replied.

He nodded in agreement.

The cadets bantered amongst themselves, all curious about the 'thing from the sky' and wanting to know more about it.

Cadet Xiao watched the dark star-object move up and down

in the water. Ensign Han Xing was on duty, collecting samples from the rock, tinkering away at the apparently tough exterior skin. It looked metallic. There were two British men, about the same age as Han Xing, helping him. Han Xing was more gentlemanly than those louts, even though he could be so arrogant. She had also seen him eyeing her a few times. She was eighteen, a maiden—but she was not going to let girlish emotions interfere with her duty.

The two British ensigns were talking animatedly while making sure the rowboat did not drift away from their center of attention. She wondered what London looked like, felt like. What she had heard and seen (from paintings) was a city filled with tall buildings, cramped streets, and beautiful gardens. Pretty much like the main capital Beijing with its cobbled walkways and small lanes. The women were apparently stylish with pretty dresses and fashionable hairdos.

Something caught her eye. A light. No, a glow, as if from the sun. It came from the rock. The three young men had noticed it too and seemed transfixed by it.

Her head throbbed. It felt as if she was having a relapse of the seasickness. She did not vomit though. Instead the throbbing continued; she felt as if there was a sound, like a high-pitched scream, emanating from the rock. She looked around worriedly and saw that her friends were also experiencing the same discomfort, their foreheads creased in pain. She flung an anxious glance at Han Xing and his companions. They were rowing desperately *away* from the rock and one of the British ensigns was retching into the sea.

It was at this moment the world turned blindingly white.

Admiral Wu came to, leaning against the helm. Nausea. She swallowed hard and pulled herself up slowly but firmly. Next to her, Tsang was having the same struggle.

What just happened? There was a blinding flash of light and the world became *white*, blanking out everything. There was also the strange sound—

"Han Xing!" She gasped and spotted the rowboat with the three boys unconscious in it. The rock was still there, a dark lodestone of untold . . . menace.

They managed to rescue the three young officers. The *Wolfhound* rushed its ship's physician over. While her own medical officer and his counterpart mulled over the boys, Wu made sure that everyone was accounted for and all right. Many showed signs of nausea and disorientation.

Someone was running up the stairs leading to the helm. Wu realized that it was Cadet Xiao; the girl's face was drained of blood and she was in an obvious state of panic.

"My lord," Cadet Xiao rasped out. She had tears in her eyes. "Madam. The rest are gone!"

"Who are gone?" Wu said firmly, shaken by the abject fear in the girl's voice.

"My friends . . . the other cadets! They just vanished! One moment they were standing next to me and then they were gone!" Xiao blurted out and started sobbing, clearly traumatized.

Wu did not like what was happening in front of her. The situation was getting progressively worse. Captain Richard Harper had appeared on deck and was demanding an explanation. Did the *Wolfhound* suffer the same white light and the resultant physical disorientation?

While one of her assistants comforted the distraught girl, Wu turned her attention to Harper whose face was similarly pale *and* angry.

"What in blazes just happened?!" he roared and Wu frowned, disconcerted and displeased at the captain's loss of emotional control.

"A bizarre occurrence. There was a strong piercing sound and many of my officers lost consciousness," she said truthfully. Harper looked as if he needed a stiff drink.

"So did *Wolfhound,*" Harper rubbed his face slowly, perturbed. "At least Jenkins and Smith are responding well to Doctor Halwell's treatment."

Wu was worried about Han Xing who was still out from it. She was also worried about the fallen star. Its status was now lifted to 'Dangerous Item'. Is it sentient? Is it alive? What *is* it?

—Then there was *music.*

Beautiful celestial-sounding music, with qin. Voices too, laughter and singing.

Harper's mouth fell open. Wu looked up and stared.

What Wu saw were seven young women and they wore the faces of the seven missing cadets. Dancing in the sky, these young women were dressed in flowing silks in the colors of dawn. Their laughter was merry and infectious and otherworldly. Straight from legends of the celestial place.

"Who are you?" Wu said, finally finding her voice. "Who *are* you? What have you done with my cadets?"

The laughter grew louder, even cheerful, sounding as if the girls were out on a lark, a leisurely stroll in the gardens. Wu narrowed her eyes and smelled something afoot. She had been in the Navy long enough to sense falsehood and danger.

"Whatever you are doing, let the girls go," she demanded coldly. "They are innocents."

"We serve a purpose," the seven maidens chorused in unison. "We are the Pleiades sisters and we are here." They were speaking *Putonghua*, the state-sanctioned Mandarin Chinese.

"Why?" Admiral Wu hissed, feeling the anger build up inside her. *How dare they?* "Why are you here?"

"We are visiting this earthly plane," one with the face of Chu, clothed in peach, answered.

"We have been watching you," one with the face of Ling, piped in.

"We are the Pleiades," one bearing the visage of Ouyang, announced, repeating the message. They spoke in riddles and Wu grew more and more frustrated.

"Let the girls go," a masculine voice joined in and it was Harper coming up beside Wu. His eyes sparked with anger and his voice was hoarse with controlled rage. Wu lifted an eyebrow in surprise. Either he understood Mandarin Chinese or the entities were somehow able to make comprehension possible.

"Why?" The question came back, taunting them.

Arrogant. It was going nowhere. The entities were . . . *entities.* Either from the rock or conveying messages from the rock, Wu did not know and did not want to make further guesses. Not now, when the situation was tense and the lives of seven girls hung on the balance. She was not the type to believe in celestial visitors.

They belonged to the realm of stories and legends, something to beguile children. Just like Chang'Er and the moon. Just like Hou Yi and his bow. Was she going to be fooled by beings from a *constellation?*

She was a trained diplomat as well as a naval officer. There were times that she dreaded using force and aggression. She knew that Harper was going through the same dilemma.

"Let them go," Wu said. "Please state what you want from us."

There was momentary silence as if there was some deliberation going on. The seven sky maidens hung voiceless, like marionettes, in mid-air. Then the one with Wang's features spoke:

"Let us go. You are not ready for enlightenment yet."

The answer was cryptic and infuriating. *Ready for enlightenment?* Wu snarled inwardly. "Do you mean we should leave that rock alone?"

"Yesssssssss." The seven maidens replied altogether, their mouths moving in harmony. In other times, Wu might have thought that the whole situation was eerie. But she was becoming cold with anger.

Why you pompous, conceited ... non-earthly entity. Wu had enough of its trickery. She hated to be treated like some errant silly child. She turned deliberately to Navigator Deng who gaped foolishly at the seven flying figures. "Prepare for flight. Inform the engine room."

"Admiral!" Deng's eyes were doubtful, but he dutifully relayed the commands by hitting the signal-chimes before him. Soon, the *Feng Huang* began her transformation from sea-faring vessel to an aerial ship, valves and doors closing in the ship's insides, pouring water from the ballast, so that it could be air-worthy. The ship clanked and shifted gears, added large vanes along aft, reduced the emission of smoke and channeled more energy to the boilers. Wu stood through the entire change from sea vessel to air-ship silent, keeping an eye on the 'Pleiades sisters'.

Harper grinned roguishly and grimly at her. "I would have done that too." The *Caesar*-class *Wolfhound* was also capable of flight since the nations were all pushing for air superiority.

As the *Feng Huang* began to lift clear from the water, her dragon bow glistening with moisture and her steam engine powering her ascent, Wu made orders to have the guns focused on the dark gleaming rock. Standing nearby, Commander Tsang realized that it was a game of bluff and she did not say anything else. Her head was still ringing from the unnatural music.

The seven maidens began to show signs of distress, wailing away, as if whatever or whoever was behind them was experiencing a certain degree of consternation.

"You expect us to sit down quietly and, suck our thumbs like little children?" Wu said coolly and she thought then of her little son in her family home. His pink-colored cheeks and happy smile. His boundless curiosity. She pushed that thought away. Put her emotions away as firmly, as coldly as possible. "You expect us to be obedient and *just let you go*?"

Seven voices started to rise in volume, higher and higher. The song seemed to go straight into the bone, drilling right into the skull.

"*Shut up*," Wu snapped irritably, and the seven voices ceased their unearthly wailing immediately. She had had enough of this entity masquerading as heavenly beings, putting her cadets in instant jeopardy. "Shut up. You have already hurt my crew. And if you hurt the seven girls, I will make sure that you will be let go, in a dazzling fashion."

The wind whispered past her, swirling around her in eddies. The *Feng Huang* was air-borne, her guns directed squarely at the alien visitor.

"Let me go," the girl with the face of Ming said in a subdued voice. "I will let the girls go, unharmed."

"Do it now," Admiral Wu stated sternly.

The music died down. The glow dimmed and the seven maidens were gently lowered onto the deck, their celestial façade gone, clad only in their normal dress uniforms.

"Admiral," Deng said suddenly. "The rock is moving."

Indeed it was, shooting up from the water, glowing brightly, sending a spray of surf into the air. It ascended into the heavens, seemingly in a hurry to get away.

"Ah," Wu said finally. "All bluff."

She then ordered the physician to check on the seven girls who were by now stirring from their unusual possession experience, expressions of confusion on their faces.

❧

Captain Richard Harper imbibed the hot jasmine tea in tiny sips, calming his nerves. They had both retired into her executive room. Wu resisted the temptation to grab a betel nut or two; instead, she drank her tea demurely and watched the British captain.

"By Jove, you deal like a man," Harper commented, putting his cup down.

Wu chuckled. "Wouldn't you have done the same thing when such anomalies threaten the safety of your crew?"

Richard grinned ruefully. "I didn't expect the whole ship to *fly*. Should have shot the blighter there and then."

"Vantage point," she smiled, this time warmly. "Surely you have learned about it in *your* academy?"

The British captain laughed.

After Harper had left for his ship, Wu made sure she visited the seven girls in the infirmary. They were still drowsy from the medication Doctor Hu had prescribed for them, but no adverse side effects from the possession. Now, how was she going to write that report?

Xiao hovered worriedly in the infirmary. This experience would linger long in her memories. She thanked Wu though, profusely and gratefully, hero-worship shining in her eyes.

It was with some degree of exhaustion Wu headed for the executive office, her mind dwelling on the technicalities of reporting the whole incident. She paused in front of the door, feeling a sudden weakness in her knees. Perhaps she needed to go back to Zhejiang, to see her family and hold her son. She was long overdue for rest.

"Mei Tzu," Tsang appeared from nowhere and Wu glanced at her friend tiredly. The commander was using her given name, indicating a level of trust and friendship. She gave Tsang a wan smile and nothing else. The first officer was holding a velvet bag and Wu recognized it immediately with a start of her heart.

"Han Xing?" The admiral opened the door and walked in slowly, feeling the aches in her shoulder blades. *Too much tension in one day.*

"He is recovering," Tsang replied, herself looking no better. She had her own reports to write. "He gives you this though."

Wu handled the bag and looked at the contents.

"You are not ..." Wu said incredulously. "These ... Zhao Jun?"

"From that *thing*. We managed to get the samples."

"Now this is going to make the whole situation very interesting. Not to mention vexing. How are we going to explain to them that the rock flew away and the retrieval mission was for naught?"

"True," Tsang chuckled wryly. "The rock, though, did threaten the ship ..." She grimaced at the recent memory. "How about Captain Harper? How is *he* going to write about this episode?"

"We are going to report the same thing. With different embellishments based on individual interpretation, of course."

Tsang tactfully slipped away, leaving Admiral Wu to step into her office, for a moment of much needed peace. The room felt comfortable. The canary clock ticked and made soft metallic noises as the springs spun, telling time. There was still the smell of jasmine. Everything was normal, routine. However, what she had experienced with her crew and the *Wolfhound*'s, was nothing short of extraordinary. How was she going to do the experience justice? Writing the report as objectively and truthfully as she could was her main task now. The sequence of events spun in her mind, like a delicate spider-web of connections and patterns. The trick was to use the appropriate words. She had the physical evidence in the form of black obsidian shards. She had no doubt that the brass would pursue the matter, especially when it concerned the seven cadets . . .

Her truth. Her crew's truth. Harper's truth. The girls' truth. Different opinions, same event. She was not a person prone to dishonesty or lying. With a sigh, she began the difficult task of writing the report with a quill pen and parchment paper, the stenograph being not in use as Ensign Han Xing was still resting in his cabin. She was an impeccable officer of the Aero-Nautical Navy and she had a job to do. She started the report by stating her rank and her full name.

Perhaps, in the end, it all boiled down to a matter of possession.

—fin—

Growing Up

Rebel in a secret war

Like a rebel in a secret war, I wrote.

While I pursued my studies in Western Australia, I continued writing. In fact, I *grew up* writing in Australia. By then, I was heavily influenced by fantasy and science fiction. I wrote my first serious chapter detailing the life of a red dragon, replete with a beguiling landscape of canyons and magic. I enjoyed my first open mic poetry reading. I explored fanfiction, I sent my first submission to an anthropomorphic zine. I loved seeing my name on paper.

My first language is English. I do not write in Mandarin Chinese, even though a part of me thinks I should. *I am Chinese, am I not?* But the language I grew up with and am most comfortable with is English. When I write, it is in English, except for the smatterings of half-hazy Mandarin Chinese, Cantonese and Hokkien words. My writing voice is English. I think and speak in English.

At first, I wielded my pen like the rebel I was *(still am, by the way—a little, I swear!)*. English became a shining blade. I wrote more, perhaps to prove to my parents that I could write well. I wrote more and my command of Mandarin Chinese grew cobwebs, became rusty and eventually atrophied. I thought I could burn bridges and set myself free.

As a diasporic Chinese, I straddle multiple worlds. I often
say that I am a textual healer. I walk between worlds; I cross
the bridges. Sometimes, one world is louder, more evocative,
than the others. And when that world speaks, it is vital to pay
attention to it.

In the beginning

I grew up with white snakes, fox women, spider ladies and a
cosmology populated with the Jade Emperor, peach fairies and
eighteen hells. At the same time, I grew up with tales of other
people, tales that became part of my life: hantu, spirit tigers and
jinn.

Growing up meant straddling between being Chinese and
being in a tropical land so different from where my ancestors
had come. My grandparents came from China, drawn by the
prospect of a better life in Nanyang. They brought along with
them traditions, customs and stories. They settled down, sank
down roots like the banyan tree and their children grew up with
the stories of many worlds.

When I first explored the world of SFF (and I didn't even
know what SFF was), it was through the fantastic landscapes
of wuxia and Chinese legends. Gallant swordsmen, daring
warrior women, amazing plotlines filled with intrigue, fighting
and extraordinary beings filled with extraordinary skills,
both physical and magical. Condor heroes, magical blades,

mythological entities come to life. The Monkey King travelled to the West, beset by myriad bewildering creatures. Dragons were sinuous, graceful and powerful controllers of water. Fairies were both benevolent and capricious. Interwoven were the customs and traditions of the Han Chinese like the Lunar New Year, Duan Wu and Mid-Autumn. The importance of family wove throughout these traditions.

Growing older, wuxia was joined by a host of other worlds. I read Anne McCaffrey's Pern books, Dragonlance and Frank Herbert's mystical *Dune*. When I was a teenager, dragons with bat wings and vicious breath took the place of the elegant sinuous dragons I knew as a child. There were starships, there were robots, and there were new worlds I could explore. There was the Star Trek dictum: Infinite Diversity in Infinite Combinations (IDIC). That was what made SFF so powerful: the possibilities, the sheer diversity.

For Singaporeans, the teen years are years filled with rigorous curriculums, where academia is paramount, where kids are pigeonholed into nice little categories. Everyone is pushed to excel and conform. Writing became my sanctuary. I would sit down at my desk and enter worlds of dragons and shape-shifters. Writing became my voice. I spoke through my prose. I remember writing my first novella (I didn't know what a novella was—it was the early nineties and there was no Internet to tell me!) and getting it read by my best friend, another Pern fan. Imagine: my first reader. My first audience. It was a powerful boost to my self-esteem.

My mother, however, didn't like the idea of me being a writer. In a fit of rage, she tore my writing and flung them in my face. My heart ripped apart with it. I sobbed and hated my mother.

So, I became a rebel. A *writer*.

Starting to remember and remembering

I paid attention. Oh boy, I did.

I remembered the worlds of poet-swordsmen and feisty women warriors. They had faces similar to mine. They spoke a language I intimately knew. I remember reading—and strange how memories become so clear like spring water—a book about valiant generals who could turn into tigers, about phoenixes; my inherent cosmology, but it was buried within me.

I remembered the stories, the morals. Chinese legends and myths teach as well as fascinate. They teach Confucian values like filial piety, honor and love for country. The customs and traditions teach about the importance of family and kin as well as the lunar passage of time. Values that resonate for me. Like a DNA strand, spiralling deep down inside me. The tales with important values intertwined with similar stories from Western traditions. I cannot separate these two strands. They are one within me. I need both. I need the bridges. I love writing. I have accepted what I am: a border-crosser, a textual healer.

Now, I smile when I see wuxia series on TV. I smile when I see stories with Chinese dragons who change shape into human form. And I smile when I see re-interpretations of the *Journey to the West.* With the advent of CGI, wuxia has become more fantasy in texture and appearance.

I return gratefully to the worlds of the Ramayana and the Mahabharata. To the stories of self-sacrifice, of love and—most importantly—of intense emotions *(that's what makes stories tick, isn't it?).* I listen to the spine-chilling tales of the pontianak, scary ghost women who died during childbirth. I listen to the tales of spirit tigers who haunt the graves of long-dead sultans. Singapore has a thriving horror fan-base, fed by a series of ghost-written (pun intended) anthologies and often-whispered ghost stories.

After years of living in Singapore and growing up with these classics and legends, I see SFF as diverse and multi-faceted. And because I straddle between so many worlds, SFF is perfect for daydreamers and writers like me. SFF is beyond English or Mandarin Chinese: it is *universal.*

Glossary:

> *hantu:* Malay for ghost.
>
> *wuxia:* The genre of Chinese martial movies (media: television series, movies and comics).
>
> *Nanyang:* Literally 'south sea'. Southeast Asia.

A Basketful of Figs

There is a fig tree in the center of our family courtyard. It has been with our family for generations, providing basketfuls of sweet-fleshed figs year after year. Celebrations are held under its peridot shade—announcements, birthdays, weddings and baby's full moons. Even festivals, all based on the waxing and waning of the moon and the transitions of the seasons. Gifts have been made, exchanged and opened while the leaves rustle their gentle song. Laughter and dancing mingle with grief and pain.

It is a medium-sized tree with a thick trunk and heart-shaped leaves, spreading outward to form an umbrella. *Ficus carica*, under the *Moraceae* family. Wu hua guo. I love the sound of it, rolling it with my tongue and savoring the texture of the words with my senses. The taste of the figs is often accentuated by the enjoyment of the word-sounds—I am the only one in my family who can taste words and I cherish my little gift. Of course, when I bite into the pinkish heart of a ripe fig, nobody knows the joy, except myself.

Oh, the edible fig tree is an interesting plant, its fruit polli-nated by the fig wasp and considered a *flower*, an *inflorescence*. Fruit without flower. How miraculous it is. We collect basketfuls on good years, providing sustenance to the entire household. We eat them fresh, dry them or preserve them for later culinary or festive use. We sometimes serve them to relatives and guests during the New Year period, accompanied by fragrant jasmine tea and tasty family gossip. Or we boil them into herbal concoctions for the soothing of sore throats and strained vocal cords.

Then the war comes and everything changes.

It is the Sino-European Territory War and it is 2376.

A long time now, China has asserted herself as a World Power, having annexed several key countries, including pretty much all of Southeast Asia and some parts of Africa. The annexation had been done way before I was born and when I was growing up, China was already powerful.

I am the descendent of Chinese immigrants. My ancestors migrated to Southeast Asia in the late 19th century and set down roots in humid tropical countries so different from their temperate homeland. It wasn't until the 22nd century that one branch of the large family I belong to decided to go back to China and re-establish themselves as a clan. The Chinese government calls us "returnees". It always makes me feel like an alien, like something out of old science fiction movies with adorable ETs. Besides the word tastes like hard plastic and it leaves a bad taste in my mouth and mind.

We flourish with the peace and stability. My great-great-grand-father planted the fig tree with a fig fruit apparently brought over from his garden back in Singapore. The fig tree grows as we grow as a family, in size. We are a mélange of people, Chinese with other races thrown in because the 20th-21st centuries saw a period of inter-marriages. I myself have blue eyes and black hair, brown skin and a Chinese name with the direct translation of Little Peace. The name I give myself is Cassidy, Cass for short.

The war comes suddenly, with a proliferation of arms, angry words and broken treaties. Somehow, one of the Federated European Union countries has found that it is sharing a tenuous (and economically fertile) border with China and has raised a political ruckus about it. There is a spate of weapon technology, a lot of saber rattling and posturing between the governments. Someone utters the wrong word and all reason is lost.

We have spent days preparing our household for the war, stocking the bunkers with sufficient supplies of food (vacuum-sealed, canned and preserved) and water (bottled and expensive). The fighting seems to be concentrated outside, near the border areas. The threat of aerial bombing is very real, because we can hear squadrons making fly-pasts over the city. We attempt to send messages to relatives living in China and elsewhere like Singapore and the neo-ASEAN states. The mood is nerve-wracking, tense. I *hate* the feeling.

Cass,

I am so grateful that you wrote. I feel as if I am living in a vacuum. We have been having daily bomb raids and I am actually quite surprised that the electricity supply is still working. I think they are trying to make us afraid. You know, make us submit and such.

Why is there a border dispute? We should be civilized citizens of the 24th century. But no, politicians are politicians.

Argh. I am sorry if I sounded angry. I am. At the whole situation. I hope you are well. Send my love to your family.

Ash.

A loud rumble, like thunder, shakes me awake early in the morning. Except that the thunder vibrates from ground up and causes everything to wobble on shelves and tables. Then there is the strong smell of burning and I am out of the bed, joining the rest of my family stumbling out of our respective rooms. Mother and Father clutch at each other as they make their way to the family bunker, leading us there, trying hard not to show fear.

The burning smell and the rumbling are the most startling and vivid outside, and I dart a frightened glance at the fig tree. It is standing firm, unwavering. I take heart from the sight of its resilient trunk and heart-like leaves, and scoop my littlest sister into my embrace as we navigate through the dawn darkness.

Morning brings relief and horror. The words coming forth from my parents' mouth taste of ash and sharp iron nails. The bombs have destroyed a few houses down our street and we can hear the wail of sirens and people in shock. I clamp my hands over my ears, trying to shut the noise out. My sisters and brothers are sobbing. Do sad words taste like salty tears?

While the family tries to recuperate with *How dare they?* and *Are we all okay?*, I find myself huddling down, knees tucked to my chest, under the fig tree. It is almost summer now and there is promise of fruit in the tree. I play with some unripe ones beside me, enjoying their waxy texture with my fingers. They must have fallen during the bomb raid.

I am nineteen and suddenly deathly afraid of the outside world. I wonder how the Alien races would perceive us, like the sanctimonious Teveri in their lofty United Nations And Planets Council seats.

Ash,

They bombed our street! The Lees have their house destroyed overnight and they are now staying with us. Mother and Father are kind enough to take them in. I see a constant stream of people coming to our house for some hot plain congee and pickled cabbage hearts. Some of them simply sit under the tree and stare into space, holding their cups of hot tea. It is heartbreaking to watch and we are just in the early days of the war?skirmish?border dispute?

I can't write for long. We are using generators here. So much for 24th century technology! Father keeps on saying that he is going to use the solar panels . . .

Take care. Remember to write (if you have time and the electricity).

Hurriedly,

Cass

Somehow or other, our family house has become an important "base". I roll the word in my mouth: concrete, tasteless. *Awful.* Refugees turn up at our doorstep and Mother takes them in. Soldiers from the Army decide to set up a communications center, right smack in the middle of the courtyard, under the fig tree. They are sweet enough not to move their bulky metallic equipment around too much. The whole place reminds me of a marketplace. A sad marketplace, with no wares to be sold and with only stricken expressions, accompanied with jerky and pained body language, as people try to comprehend what is happening to them and around them. The words I hear are not delicious or savory words. I try to ignore them, but I end up tasting them, *remembering* them. It is pungent like the bitter dark herbal teas, composed of bark, root and other plant parts, that Mother makes all the time to alleviate disharmony and imbalance in bodily yin or yang. And as children, we always remember the bitterness most keenly.

I am put in charge of feeding the refugees and the displaced. Mother and First Aunt get up every morning to prepare the large pots of rice congee, adding only salt for taste and stirring it frequently so that it reaches a creamy consistency. The soldiers try to ensure a steady supply of rice for us and they help out too, carrying the bags of rice on their bronzed shoulders. They are all about my age, perhaps slightly older. University-age young men.

The fragrance of cooking congee seems to instill a sense of normalcy and routine. I dish out bowls of hot congee quietly and dutifully. It is a comforting pattern and people cling to patterns, especially when their worlds are thrown into chaos. While I hand the bowls out, I struggle with my own internal conflicts. I want to go to university and read botany. I want to do so many things. The war has affected us, put a stop to anything.

There is a young soldier by the name of Benjamin I end up talking to all the time. He is fresh-faced, his dark hair cut close to his skull. I notice his eyes: they are aquamarine. He speaks fluent Bahasa, a wonderful language that I relish and love, a gift from my Peranakan grandmothers. He is also the son of immigrants from immigrants. He speaks clear flowing Mandarin, the pu-tong-hua of the Chinese government. His words taste like magic.

When my chores are done, I would sit under the fig tree and he would come over to join me. We sip the hot congee slowly and pretend that there is no war, no danger. Just the soft rustle of fig leaves and bird song. It is firmly summer now and the heat permeates everything, even through clothes. I can see ripening fruit, singles, clusters of them, hanging on the tree. Would there be a basketful of figs this year?

"So you taste words?" Benjamin asks me, his eyes sparkling. *Like the sea*, I muse. His words are warm amber honey, smooth and fluid down my throat.

"Yes," I reply, staring at the milky congee, unsure of what or how to feel. I might have come across to him as feminine. Indeed, I was born a girl. Yet, I feel more masculine inside. Perhaps, I am androgynous. Oh, all the conflicts of youth.

I am acutely conscious of his gaze.

"I think it is called synaesthesia ," he says and I nod, already aware of the term. The word tastes like acidic sweet lemon fizz on my tongue. He is trying to make small talk and in this tumultuous time, I welcome it.

Soon he is called away to man the communications equipment and I am left alone, under the sheltering tree.

Cass,

Oh my god, they just declared full-scale war. [BLOCKED COUNTRY NAME] *is not going to relent, in spite of the UNAPC's warnings.* [ERROR] *I can't write a lot, because I think they are monitoring our messages. Not sure by who and which side though.* [ERROR] [SCAN USER/SENDER]

This war is all screwy, unpleasant and disgusting. [ERROR]

Ash [CONFIRM USER/SENDER?]

Ash,

I got your message. I am seeing a lot of missing words. Even our words have become suspect. You do know me and my thing about words. [ERROR] *Words have power. They want to take that away from us.* [ERROR]

I want this war to go away. Perjuangan nyah!

Infuriated and Sad,

Cass [CHECK RECIPIENT/LOCATION]

I am not going to take sides. The whole thing has devolved into a war of words and weapons, a sort of "He says" and "She says", except it is only on a more global (and dangerous) scale, because other nations and countries have been dragged into this ... confrontation. I wish I have clear spring water with me so that I can cleanse my palate. The words ... *hurt.*

I am seeing more refugees now. The bombing has become more severe. They are building a *camp* around my family house. Now my family, my clan, is inevitably and irrevocably involved.

Benjamin begins to look more haggard. *Harried.* His brilliant aquamarine eyes are dull, listless. I hear snatches of voices—angry, panicking, desperate—coming from the communications equipment. The words sting like sharp electric shocks in my mouth. I feel sorry for him. He tells me that he wants the war to end too.

Summer Solstice arrives, subdued and uncelebrated. The heat is unforgiving, relentless. The fig tree does not resound with laughter and warm conversation. Instead I see desolation. We are now seeing more wounded people and their injuries add a sour and painful tone to the atmosphere. The army medics work together with Fourth Aunt who is a trained nurse, seeing to the patients and performing triage on new arrivals.

Yet I am not going to give up. While the camp swirls around me, *pain/agony/loneliness* a persistent undercurrent throbbing in the air, I pick a wicker basket from the kitchen and stroll, quite casually, to the fig tree. While people watch, including Mother, Father and the rest of my family, I begin to harvest the ripe figs. Benjamin soon joins me. Then Mother and Father. My sisters hesitate at first before tentatively reaching up and plucking the figs off the branches. Some of the refugees pitch in as well, climbing onto ladders to reach the ones at the top. They smile happily as they harvest the figs.

The basket fills quickly. I stand back and look at the figs, unable to say anything. Someone—*Benjamin?*—drapes a warm arm around my shoulder and tears roll from my eyes. Salty water curving down my cheeks, curling off my jaw-line. I have a feeling that the harvest would be the last. The floodgates open and I sob. Susah hati. My heart splits open and spills forth its blood.

That night I find myself in the arms of Benjamin. We make tender love, two lonely souls in the midst of war trying to seek comfort.

[FROM UNDISCLOSED LOCATION: DDTHXBW]

Cass,

If you are reading this by now, my family house is already damaged and we are fleeing on foot. Looters have smashed all the fleeter-cars. The roads are jammed with people. I am writing this on my DISK. Hooray for hand-held comps and personal self-will/tenacity!

I love you, Cass. May we meet at the end of the journey. [ERROR]

Berani mati,

Ash

[STATIC—SEARCH FOR USER/SENDER]

The loss of my closest cousin weighs heavily on my heart and yet I find myself unable to cry. My tear-ducts seem to have run dry, after the harvest of the figs. How am I going to mourn the dead when I know, somewhat, that she might still be alive? On the run, no doubt, but alive and kicking . . . somewhere?

Benjamin is a silent pillar of strength, even though he looks wan and distraught. He tries to smile and reassure me. But I know. The war is not going well. The other side is winning.

Our lovemaking is a salve, a sacred act, witnessed only by the silent fig tree who shields us with her buttress roots. The crushed fig leaves perfume our mat with the scent of green sap and I always wake with a leaf or two stuck to my hair.

I am going to cut my hair one of these days. I will make that transition.

The first Marauder tanks have roared in. Spiky metal beasts with large cannons mounted. These cannons bring death. The news speak of their wake of destruction, of buildings blown apart and crushed, of people fleeing for their lives or buried under tons of rubble.

I can hear fighting now. Rattling of guns. Loud explosions. Strange that for the 24th century, we are still reliant on guns and grenades. I know the Teveri think we are enfants terribles. Children trying to pretend they are adults and failing horribly. And it is not at all strange that they have not even intervened or said anything.

Because it is Earth's war, not theirs. They would rather keep their claws clean rather than have them sullied by a war not their own.

Armed soldiers now surround the camp and within—my family. Mother and Father try to cheer everyone up—the soldiers, the refugees and our family—with songs and tales from our family archives. For a moment, there is a festive spirit in the courtyard with Father stringing the lanterns across the courtyard, reminiscent of Mid-Autumns long past. The lanterns glow red and orange, adding color and life to the dullness of the camp. Someone has brought out a guitar and strums familiar tunes. Another person plays the flute. A girl beats a Middle-Eastern rhythm on her dombek. People get up from their mats and beds to dance to the simple music.

Third Aunt brings out the preserved figs and we share the sweetmeats amongst ourselves, amongst the soldiers and the refugees. We also eat the present batch of figs. Fresh. Sweetness fills my mouth, replenish my memories. I eat the figs, just as I eat the words I hear floating around me. Words of comfort. Words of hope. Words of worry and anxiety. Words. The *rat-tat-tat* of gunfire punctuates the air and still I savor the figs, the words and the intimacy of family. Ikatan keluarga. Ties that bind.

Of course I do not expect the Teveri to swoop in and rescue us in our hour of need. The fighting sounds closer and closer now. The lanterns flicker in the breeze, causing some to look up anxiously, ready to light the candles again.

And while we celebrate and sing, the fig tree stands firm and resolute, its leaves speaking its own courage, its roots its strength. It has lived for generations. It will live on.

[FROM UNDISCLOSED LOCATION: GZBNRQJ]

Ash,

They invaded our city. Our family house is gone. I am on the run now, with Mother and Father. First and Third Aunts did not make it. The mortar bombs crushed the roof they were under. I am using a portable Speak-Ease and I hope you receive the message, wherever you are. If you are alive.

Are you still alive?

It is all gone. Even the fig tree. I thought it would survive. It was so strong and had withstood the test of time. But the first mortar fell right on top of it and blew it into pieces. There are broken branches, bark and fruit everywhere. Splinters hurting and, piercing our bodies. I still need to get the splinter out of my right arm. We are running and there is no time to rest.

The Teveri are no help at all. They are probably laughing at Earth's follies. What fools we are!

Benjamin is dead. He died defending the camp. You don't know about him. But he was there when I needed comfort. He was a soldier trying to defend what and whom he loved. He was a "returnee", just like you and me. Immigrant's descendant. Like our families. You don't know him. I love him and he's now gone. Dua sejoli tidak menyanyi. My joy is gone.

I cut my hair. I now look like a boy and I will probably stay that way until the war ends and after. I hope you like this aspect of me. I miss you. A lot.

And oh, I have kept some of the figs. Do you remember eating them? We used to harvest them together. The figs are in my pocket now. I want to grow them, watch them flourish. Peace will come back. I pray it will. We will return to our homes soon.

Till we meet again, Ash.

A lot of love,

Cass.

```
[END OF MESSAGE] <static> [END OF MESSAGE]
```

Glossary:

Perjuangan nyah:	Go away war!
Berani mati:	Not afraid of death.
Dua sejoli tidak menyanyi:	Lovebirds will never sing.
Ikatan keluarga:	Family ties.
Susah hati:	Uneasy/pained.

—fin—

The Sound of Breaking Glass

The present.

Well, this is it.

I see. It looks *old*. Sure it's the right place?

I double-checked. Unit 1-10.

Wonder if he's in or not.

Looks like he's not. Nobody's answering the door.

Is he seriously batshit crazy? A bit siao. I mean, all the junk outside. Some are positively ancient. Fire hazard, definitely. All the newspapers are already yellow!

He's just a little eccentric, that's all. I mean, he's harmless.

The neighbors say that they keep hearing the sound of breaking glass at night. That's why they called us. They don't want people to get hurt. He's obviously a hoarder. Not sure if he's violent.

⁕⁕⁕

The neighbors also say that he likes hanging wind chimes made of glass bits on the black wattle trees outside the apartment block. Colorful glass bits, mind you, made of broken glass bottles and fishing string.

Okay, the door is slightly ajar. Want to go in? We are volunteers, right? Ladies first.

It is so dark and musty. And what am I seeing? *Wait.* Glass bottles. Look, Cedric, just look at all these glass bottles. Different colors. Green, blue, red, transparent. He must have collected them from the coffee shops and the dumpsters. So many bottles.

Ouch. I seem to have stepped into glass shards. Oh wow. He really polishes them, doesn't he? All the sharp edges gone. So smooth, like pebbles.

He must have been a glass smith or something when he was a young man . . . Just look at these wind chimes. They glow in the light. Peridot green, sea blue, ruby red. And the music they make. Magical.

Someone once told me that he hangs them out to entertain the fairies. Or spirits. Either way. Really weird stuff.

They are just wind chimes, Cedric. Very charming. I mean, he's obviously *talented*. Why doesn't he sell them or something? Why does he want to remain a karang guni man?

Maybe he just wants to remain a karang guni man to collect weird things and entertain fairies as a hobby?

Cedric, you are so—Wait, I see something. Oh god, Cedric, come over here. You have to see this.

Shit. I think he must have been dead for one day or two. I am going to call the police.

I think he tripped, Cedric, and couldn't get up. There is dried blood on the floor. Head injury. Oh god, this is so—

Calm down, Ling. I called the police. They are arriving in about 5 mins. They are bringing the ambulance too.

It's already too late, Cedric. Too late.

Outside the unit, the wind chimes stir in the breeze, twinkling in the twilight, inviting the fairies and other spirits to sing with them.

The music the chimes make is not the sound of breaking glass, but a gentle tinkle, almost like laughter born of a light heart freed from sorrow and bleeding hands.

A few years ago.

He found the fairy entangled up in wire netting designed to trap birds.

It was a quiet afternoon, warm because it was the dry and hot season, and quiet because he lived in an apartment block filled mostly with men and women of his age. The sunlight was an uncomfortably bright orange, coating the brick walls with a glare. The trees rustled—fruit trees: starfruit, belimbing and jambu. He knew it was warm, because even the mynahs that feasted on the ripe and unripe bounty were conspicuously absent.

He was coming back from the neighborhood coffee shop, carrying his load of used aluminum cans and glass bottles. He had not been working for a long time now, preferring to collect newspapers, cans and glass bottles, all the disposable detritus of modern-day living to supplement his meager income. He received about fifty dollars per month from all the collected objects, enough to buy him simple daily essentials. The volunteers from the Moral Home Society would bring him food in the form of Khong Quan biscuits, Milo and instant noodles. Sometimes, the good-hearted Malay lady who fed the stray cats would bring him vegetables and fruits.

Lugging the bag filled with cans and bottles, he made his way to his unit. It was a small abode, filled with stacks of newspapers and used appliances, not yet exchanged with the companies who made money taking in recyclables. He had decided to live here, ever since his wife passed away and he chose not to live in an old folks' home. He did not want to waste away in a place designed for such. He cared not about his grown sons who had conveniently forgotten about him, except for the Lunar New Year where they made a big show lavishing him with mostly useless gifts.

At first, he thought it was a bird—a mynah or a sparrow—caught in the thin wire nets strung up by the town council to deter any pests. They often did so, after receiving complaints from irate and tidy-minded people. He sighed, dropped his bag and walked towards the nets. He loved birds.

The winged creature was struggling itself into a spin, thin leg caught in the net. Birds often died in this way and he buried them under the trees. It made no noise though, just a determined *flap-flap-flap* of wings.

He reached out to hold the bird ... only to find out that the bird was actually a little girl. Or that it looked like a little girl, clad in a peach-pink gossamer—*like spider silk,* he thought amazed—dress. She had brown sparrow-like wings attached to her back.

For a moment, he gaped and backed away. Jing. Evil spirits. He was brought up with stories like that. Fairies and spirits were not often benevolent and kind-hearted in the stories and myths. They were chaotic little beings, mischievous at best, capricious at their worst.

Now he did not like seeing living creatures—jing or animal—suffering. Not good for his karma. Indecision warred with compassion. Compassion won—and he gently removed the thin wire netting around the fairy's ankle. The fairy rubbed her ankle, soothing the abraded skin with a pained expression on her thin face.

"Wait here," he heard himself saying. "I will get some Tiger Balm for you." And so in he went, into his little dim housing unit, grabbed the half-used container from the broken shelf and hurried out, thankful that the fairy was still waiting for him. She leaned wearily against the lamppost, next to the bird trap. Her eyes were closed.

He had to dip his little pinky into the pungent minty ointment, scooped a finger-nail sized amount and applied it, ever so gently, on the reddened skin. *Even fairies get hurt,* he thought as the fairy visibly relaxed and gave a soft wince of relief. She exercised her sparrow wings and cocked her head to regard him. *Like a bird.* She looked vaguely Chinese.

"Thank you," she said in a sweet piping voice, speaking fluent Cantonese. He blinked, surprised, hearing his native tongue issuing forth from a little . . . fairy.

"Um," he uttered uncertainly and the fairy darted away, disappearing into the distance, a flash in the sunlight.

He certainly could not sleep that night, his mind filled with Cantonese-speaking fairies that looked like sparrows. Pulling himself out from bed, he began to sort the bottles out. He had a plan.

He had been a glass smith once, way back in the forties and fifties, when he was a young man, fresh from Guangzhou. He apprenticed himself to a glass smith working in one of the more rural areas (now a thriving industrial town known for metal and steel work). He liked the look of glass, how it melted under extreme heat and how it would form into various shapes. How it shone under the sun.

He did not have the tools of the glass smith now, only a rusty hammer he found discarded at the foot of the stairwell near his unit. With it, he began to break the glass bottles. He hoped the fairy and her friends liked the colors of red, blue and green. He had rejected the Guinness Stout bottles because the color of the glass was too dark, not bright enough.

Without the proper tools, his hands bled, cut by the sharp shards. He had to use sandpaper (salvaged from a carpentry shop) to smooth the vicious edges and even then, his skin bled.

Then, he used fishing string (again, from the same carpentry shop—the boss liked to do a fair bit of fishing) and threaded the glass pieces with it, looping and tying them so that they stayed secure. It was delicate work. The fishing string was thin, like the bird trap wires. He rued his clumsy fingers, no longer nimble for such fine and delicate crafting.

In the morning, he hung the first wind-chime up on the jambu tree, where he spotted yet another bird trap. The wind-chime tinkled in the morning breeze, glittering *red-blue-green-transparent* on the low hanging branch.

"Uncle," a boy stopped in his tracks, his bicycle squealing to a halt. "What are you doing?"

"Entertaining the fairies," he answered, watching the wind chime sparkle in the sun.

For every bird trap he discovered, no matter how discreet and well-hidden the officers of the town council had meant them to be, he made a glass bottle wind chime.

One evening, when he was about to make some broth out of instant noodle soup mix (the Malay lady had not visited him as she was busy with her family), the fairy appeared with another fairy. They carried, with some difficulty, a plastic bag filled with fried chicken wings. He stared as they placed it, almost reverently in front of him, before flying off laughing gaily. He cautiously peeled open the bag and the delicious aroma of freshly fried chicken plumed forth, bathing his face in oily fragrant steam.

The fairies continued to bring food every week. They carried in pok choi, string beans, chye sim and assorted root vegetables like sweet potatoes (his personal favorite—steamed or boiled) or muang kuang. He did not know how they managed to collect all these vegetables. Perhaps, they salvaged from the wet market. He was grateful for their kindness, for their generosity. In return, he made more of the glass bottle wind chimes. His hands bled but he did not care. He woke one day to find that the fairy had left him a small tube of cream for cuts and bruises.

The wind chimes seemed to capture the attention of the apartment dwellers. Children often stopped and watched the glass bits stirring in the breeze. Sometimes, they stole the wind chimes and yet he did not get angry. Instead, he made more wind chimes, breaking the glass bottles at night and tying the glass shards with fishing string.

The parents got concerned and they wrote to the town council about the weird and violent old man who broke glass at night. *Please send down police,* they requested urgently. *Or people from IMH. We are afraid he might hurt our children with his broken glass.*

Trying to placate the residents and wanting to be seen doing its job, the town council sent officers to knock on the old man's door and place warning letters under the slit, hoping he read the letters. He simply threw them away and went on making the wind chimes.

It was two days before the Hungry Ghosts' Festival when the smooth glass pebbles started appearing in little plastic bags. He had noticed his unfinished glass shards disappearing a couple of weeks ago and was concerned, because he had to make the wind chimes for the fairies. The glass pebbles intrigued him. Someone had smoothed the edges, made the glass pleasant to the touch. He made wind chimes out of these glass pebbles and hung them on trees. The music they made was different from the sharp-edged glass shards. Softer, sweeter, lighter.

Like fairy laughter.

He would sometimes catch glimpses of the wind chimes at night and how they would draw groups of stray cats who would just sit and watch the glass bits twinkle intermittently under the light of the street lamps. Or there would be small little moths fluttering close to the wind chimes, drifting like white petals in the breeze.

More letters came from the town council. He shredded them and threw them into the gunnysack designated for recycling. All this happened during the weeks within the Hungry Ghosts Month. He could hear the funeral wakes in the day and at nights,

Buddhist chants wafting in the quiet estate air. Oddly enough, he felt strangely protected and did not worry about hungry spirits haunting his abode. The food and pebbles still appeared as if on schedule and he was grateful for these little gifts.

The wind chimes are still there, singing in the breeze, serenading the fairies and warning them of secret dangers.

—fin—

The Bones Shine Through With Light

Children go to bed with the stories of the tiger demoness who eats knuckle bones like peanuts, huddling under our blankets while images of bones being crushed by huge fangs spin in our frightened minds.

The tiger demoness prowls in the shadows, a feline shadow in pools of darkness. In her human form, she is an old lady, kindly, if you don't really look too closely at her eyes. Her amber, cold, eyes. She often offers her services as a nanny to tired farmer parents. Once the deal is done, the fate of the children is sealed. While the parents work tirelessly at the rice fields, the tiger lady comes and feasts on the soft plump flesh of her charges. She keeps the knuckle bones, stores them up and eats them later.

Kerunch, kerunch, kerunch, the storyteller will always embellish the story with awful sounds. *Kerunch.* Because the tiger demoness relishes the taste, the texture. *Kerunch.*

Word came about the appearance of a strange old lady. She just turned up along the edges of Wulong village, a long figure in rags. She found residence in an abandoned rice shack. People said that they could see smoke rising forth from a hidden fire. They said that they heard strange noises from the rice shack.

Tiger demoness, they whispered in the tea houses. *Tiger demoness,* they whispered in the bustling marketplace where the dumplings steamed and candied hawthorn enticed little children.

Parents shooed their children into the safety of their houses and bade them never to wander near the demoness's rice shack.

I find myself wandering too closely to the tiger demoness's hut, my feet crunching too loudly on the fallen mulberry leaves. Late in autumn, there is a chill in the air.

I smell fire, the comforting aroma of burning wood. I also smell meat. Barbequed meat, like Old Gao's famous and mouth-watering roasted duck. I peer right through the rushes, feeling my stomach grumble with hunger. The weather turns cold, winter approaches and I grow hungry often.

Bones. A lot of bones. Hanging in clusters. Whole skeletons, all grotesque, like miniature gwei. Ghosts. The light piercing through the roof shines through the bones, making them glow. The sight is oddly beautiful.

"The bones tell me I have a visitor!"

The *voice*. Like a thunderclap, like a gentle grandmotherly caress.

I cry out in terror and scramble for my life. My heart drums like a mad festival gong.

The strange old lady was odd in her ways. She sang to bones, they said, secretly in their huts, during the dark of night. She sang to bones and they danced like puppets during Spring Festival shows.

Ach! Afterwards, she eats them! Women muttered amongst themselves when they met at the local well. *Tiger demoness! Eater of bones! Feh, feh, feh!*

I am creeping towards the old rice shack once more, thrilling and delicious danger coursing in my body. I want to know more about the old lady. I want to know about the bones alit with light. It is colder now, winter definitely closer. In the village, they are selling hot spicy dumplings that warm the body when eaten hot. The rice is now harvested. Very soon, it will be Winter Solstice.

Fire, and the smell-taste of barbequed meat in the air. There is singing, like the lullaby Mother uses to rock my little brother to sleep. It sounds so sad, so poignant.

I poke a tentative finger through the brittle rush.

She is stripping meat off bones. Cooking meat sizzles on hot coals. I watch her fingers, so gnarled and delicate, peel off the meat in red ribbons. And for a horrible moment, I know that she is going to eat the bones. Like peanuts or pumpkin seeds. *Kerunch. Kerunch. Kerunch.*

I continue to watch. The meat is making me salivate.

She is done with the bones now, carefully arranging them on the floor. Her expression.

Concentration, as if she is reading. Her eyes are closed. Her mouth moves.

A *cluck-cluck-cluck* almost scares me half to death. I look at the rooster strutting in front of me, all colorful feathers and brilliantly red floppy comb.

Would he end up being her dinner?

Lee Jian and his farmer cronies complained loudly about their missing chicken and ducks. This late in autumn, with the first frost on the ground. They needed the meat and the eggs, the latter to make salted eggs to sell in the markets and feed their families. Their families were always hungry.

Meanwhile, everyone prepared for winter. Mothers brought out the thick winter clothing and mended old garments. The village would soon become silent, covered with snow.

Children listened to the stories of tigress demonesses feasting on knuckle bones and felt hungry-sad-scared. They slept fitfully as the snow began to fall in flurries of white.

Wrapped in thick fleece, I struggle towards the rice shack. There is the smell of fire and the tantalizing aroma of roasting meat. My stomach growls.

When I peek in, she is hanging bones. They swing slightly, stirred by some invisible breeze. They are white, the color of snow. Tiny gwei. Tiny ghosts bereft of feathers and skin. She lifts one bone up, a tiny bone the size of my finger, and gazes at it. The fire in the rice shack crackles, casting jittery shadows on the rush walls. More bones, more skeletons: birds.

Don't eat the bones, don't eat the bones, I think, remembering, shivering, my skin chapped by the cold. I am hungry. Always hungry.

"I know you are outside, little girl," the old woman turns around and her smile is warm, like the fire. "Come in, come in."

Tiger demoness!

Trapped, I have no way to go. I duck into . . . a fragrant warmth, redolent of the best food I have eaten. The fire is so inviting . . .

The bones. The bones. *The bones.*

"Come, eat," the old woman gestures with a wrinkled hand, placing a stick of freshly roasted meat into my numb hand. I sniff at it. Chicken. I take one tentative bite. Soon, I am taking larger and large bites, chewing and swallowing. The juice is so sweet! I lick my fingers, hungry for more.

"Never easy being an old woman, thrown out by an unfilial son," the old woman says, sitting down wearily. I wince, listening to her knees creak alarmingly. "And food is so scarce these days.

"I take what I can," she continues, sipping something from a chipped porcelain cup. I realize most of the things she has in the rice shack are discards. She must have salvaged the cups and the plates. Here a bowl of old dumplings. There a plate of moldy-looking meat buns. And the bones. Too many bones.

She hands me another stick of meat. I eat more slowly now, intrigued by her words. Her eyes are not amber. They are a faded brown.

"You must be wondering about the bones," the old woman smiles, her teeth showing gaps. Yet her smile is genuine. A grand-mother's smile.

"I collect bones. I read bones. You know, a bone soothsayer.

The clod of a son thinks I am dabbling with evil jin and dark magic. But it runs in my family, bone reading. I know how old a thing is by looking at a bone. If you shine light through it, it glows."

Tiger demoness!

Frightened, I dare not say anything.

"You like to observe things, don't you, little one?"

I nod slowly, wonderingly. *How did she know? Did the bones tell her?*

"There is nothing to eat here," the old woman sighs. "I make do with what I have. Even the marrow inside the bones." In her hand rests a mortar stone, round with years of repeated use. She takes one chicken bone. *Kerunch.* "Try it. It's food. Nourishment. Eat." *Kerunch.*

I stare at the smashed splinters, at the dark red marrow oozing out like red bean paste. She watches me, the old lady, the tiger demoness in disguise.

The marrow tastes mealy and bloody. But so rich it fills my mouth and wakes my senses. *So rich.* I eat some more, grateful for the nourishment. *So rich and delicious.*

When spring arrived, with the festive sounds of the Lunar New Year, the old lady was gone. *Disappeared,* said the men in the tea houses. *Like magic. Like a jin.* The rice shack became just an empty hut, bereft of fire and life. She took everything.

Their chicken and ducks came back too. The farmers found their coops and backyards filled with healthy clucking fowl.

With the promise of fresh eggs and steamed chicken on New

Year tables, thoughts of tiger demonesses and bone knuckles faded away, like the soft footsteps of an old lady travelling down the melting snow.

She has taught me so many things. Bones. The stripping of bones. The reading of bones. The light shining through bones. She has taught me many secret things, things passed down from mother to daughter in her family. The bloodline ended with the birth of her son. She was getting old. She wanted to teach me.

I wanted to learn.

She has also taught me the filling of bones. Her little rice shack suddenly filled with birds. The fluttering of feathers, the noises of pecking, of strutting. The bones given life, flesh.

It was a mystery.

When I grew older, I began to collect bones too. I gazed at the bones, the candlelight turning the white translucent. They whispered to me about secret lives. Mysteries.

I know that when winter arrives, I will have nourishment and life.

—fin—

Terrain

Yao Jin

She hated the abattoir.

Her client knew it and still sent her on this merry jaunt. Perhaps he had never inhaled the smell of coagulating and frozen blood, still coppery, still rich, still with the hint of heartsblood. Perhaps he had never touched the cool skin of the formerly live animal and wanted to feed.

She cursed him to the Eighteenth Hell and padded down the stairs, mindful of her own urges. She didn't like to eat on the job. Trixie would have kept some in the fridge, just for her.

The creature was somewhere in the cold *dripping* bloody *delicious* meat factory.

Her shoulder brushed one of the handing carcasses. It moved, as if it drew breath. Indeed, she heard its breathing, like a szzztszzztszzzt.

Bloody Eighteenth Hell!

Something dark and hateful and spiky with spite hit her.

This time, she responded by letting out her urges.

Trixie was mopping the floor when she limped in through the door. She had to stop. Trixie hated getting the floor dirty. And now she was mopping the tiled floor with the passion of a scourer, one of those god-bothering devotees. Trixie wasn't a scourer. Never professed having a religion or any form of spirituality.

"Feck!" Trixie swore, dropped her mop and rushed over to her. "You are fecking injured."

"Glad you noticed," she replied. The creature got her across the chest, across her breasts. Which meant she had to loosen her binds and let Trixie treat the wound. Trixie was ex-medico.

"Feck, sit down, Amara, before you get the tiles bloody. Wait while I get the med bag."

She eased herself into one of the rickety chairs. Once she got the damned money from her client, she was going shopping, damn it. And a new jacket. The creature ruined it.

Trixie blustered out of the treatment room with her med bag. It was genuine leather, made from a bovine source and highly priced, not like the cheap humanaskin in the markets

"Feck," Trixie muttered as she carefully peeled off the thin grey camisole, fresh red blood welling up from disturbed scabs. "Feck, what didya do?"

"Fought a preta," she winced. "Hey, careful!"

"If you sit still," Trixie still had the medico voice down pat. She started cleaning up the wounds with medical alcohol. "Claws?"

"Long ones."

"Feck. Ah Long asked you to do this?"

She nodded, comforted by the concern in Trixie's soft contralto.

"Was it worth all this?" Trixie gestured at the wounds, deep gouges that even her body would take some time to heal. "All *this?*"

"I do what I am born to do."

"Feckhell, don't give me that nonsense again."

Trixie finished padding the wounds up with enough gauze

and bandage, sternly warning Amara to take care when she showered. She always gave the same lecture. The same 'Don't this' and 'Don't that' since they started the preta-hunting agency. Trixie made sure she ate. She lost precious energy after hunting preta. And preta were growing more and more in Nightshome like an infestation of lice.

The cold slabs of meat—bovine and fresh from the killing market—went down her throat in a rich thick river of *bloodbloodblood*. She savored the copper, knowing that her wounds were knitting as the blood went into her body. She sighed out of sheer pleasure.

"You are showing your fangs," Trixie said, and this time she was smiling.

⁂

The phone rang an hour before dawn. She knew, because her body was tuned to the dawn and the darkness between it. And on her off-day too. Beside her, Trixie stirred and murmured "Feckoff" before going back to sleep.

It was Ah Long. She had never seen him. His voice was all she ever knew of his existence. He belonged to the upper clans. He gave assignments and paid on time.

"Apologies for waking you up on your rest day."

Oh sure, bloody Eighteen Hell brat. "Nevermind, just give me the assignment." Outside, she heard the city stirring, just as Trixie had stirred, waking up. Steeltrains rumbled on their rail tracks. People swore and spat. She smelled the breakfast trucks. Her mouth watered.

"There is a flesh forest found at the fringes of Nightshome. I think there is a preta or more of them there. The payment will be 1,000 skulls."

1,000 skulls? Oh precious skies. We are rich.

Then her hearts sank. High pay usually meant an extremely difficult case.

She wasn't sure how she would tell Trixie. But Trixie was normal human and normal humans thought like normal humans. In flesh ways and in flesh terms. She had to keep them both fed and the agency going without tanking again.

She left Trixie still wrapped up in the blankets. She slipped out into the Nightshome morning, holding her ruined jacket close to her body. She was already shivering. Her urges were calling out to her.

Of course, she fed. She stopped by one of the meat trucks and ordered a string of hearts. She bit into the juicy organs, feeling herself grow stronger.

"Out hunting, dakini?" The seller asked. He was a familiar face.

She nodded. She couldn't resist ordering another string. They were always so sweet and delectable. She knew where he had gotten his supplies. Finishing the hearts, she turned to a beverage stall. As usual, she had her stim-tea, flavored with blood flakes. She sprinkled a liberal amount. She loved that particular spice.

Breakfast done, she began her hunt.

In the dream, she ran, clawed feet, running and flying.

In the dream, she was the hunter and she knew her prey was near.

She laughed and the whole universe laughed with her.

In one hand, she grabbed her vajira. In another hand, she held the skull bowl.

She supped deep of the skull bowl.

Her song filled the roiling skies.

Flesh forests grew regularly in Nightshome.

It wasn't Nightshome all the time. The realms changed frequently. It was the cycle of the Prayer Wheel. Soon, it would be another cycle. But that would take another hundred years or more.

Flesh forests grew, because humans died and left the corpses behind to seed the plains. The vulture-birds, the Cleaning Ones, were no longer alive. They had gone extinct when Terra died. Even planets died and she told Trixie of that truth before.

"I am no preta," Trixie had said, her eyes clouding over. Her eyes were like cirque lakes. Even those were gone when Terra trembled in her death throes. "I am . . . me."

She didn't have the hearts to tell Trixie she had found her unconscious in a life-pod.

She had to focus. Preta were hard to kill, sticking to undead and Hungry life as they did when they lived. She hated flesh forests too. They were as triggery as abattoirs. Within her, her urges howled. They always howled before the hunt. They simmered like fire lakes beneath her skin. She wore this skin to live unharmed in Nightshome.

The flesh forest had the stench of rotting flesh and the hiss of a thousand flies. Her feet, sheathed at the moment, crunched on dry scalps. The swollen bodies in various sizes and shapes of putrefaction stood like the trees of old. One, still huge with a dead fetus, had outstretched arms like branches. It bore grotesque fruits, boils the size of infested bolls along the gnarly sides.

Preta lurked in these forests.

She didn't have to wear her jacket. That too was an affectation like her name. She wasn't always Amara.

She opened her skin and let her urges, her real self out.

Trixie had seen her real self before once. That was before they founded the agency. Trixie didn't freak out. Her claim was that she had seen worse.

She had a wolf's head but with three luminous eyes. Her fur was blue, the blue of a bruise, and her claws were crescent-shaped. Her wolf's mouth was filled with dagger teeth, to shred preta and return them to truth. Her hair, the night-black hair, framed her wolf face.

Her vajira she held in her claws, its pommel a screaming dakini's head.

The preta didn't take long to emerge from the bodies. They hid there.

She slashed through them with her vaijra, taking their heads off and biting into their necks. She had forgotten about her wounds inflicted by a preta now gone to its Final Death. She hoped it would reincarnate in a better world.

They kept coming, a loathsome walking phalanx.

"Would you . . . bring us . . . to nirvana?" One hissed, corpse-breath escaping from the slit on its face. "Now? Now? Now? Would you? Would you?"

"Would you? Would you?" The rest echoed, a macabre choir.

Her vajira answered. Limbs littered the scalp-covered forest floor.

"Go to your Final Death!" She howled and the forest shook with her rage.

The killing took less than an hour. The limbs and heads piled up. She clutched their souls and flung them away, into the truth-light. They were different from the hate-thing which slashed her the day before.

When she closed her skin, she realized she was cut and bruised everywhere. The flesh forest stank even stronger now. She hadn't fed. Flesh still lingered in her mouth and she spat it out.

Trixie was going to yell at her.

The payment pinged into her credit on time. She was surprised that Trixie didn't yell at her. Just looked at her with tired eyes.

"More cuts," Trixie said. "Aiyah." She had removed her contacts and her real eye color was the color of dark chocolate. Chocolate was now rare in Nightshome. She saw gold in the darkness, like flashes of anger. "You know what the stalls called you? Yao jin. Demon."

"They can't differentiate between yao jin and dakini."

"Feck, stay still. I don't like rotting nails digging into your already stressed flesh."

The antiseptic tingled. She was grateful for Trixie's gentle touch.

"Try living as human for once."

That argument again. Trixie never gave up trying to convince her to live normally. She couldn't deny her urges.

"I am not human," she reminded Trixie. "Not once, never."

"You wear human skin and behave like one."

"I have to pass unnoticed."

Their conversation teetered towards an argument, one long overdue.

"Amara, listen. I love the agency as much as you do. But you . . . you hurting yourself every day for it . . . isn't going to work in the long term. I don't like seeing you hurt."

Ah. Human feelings. Human sentiments.

"Trixie."

"Don't 'Trixie' me," Trixie's eyes narrowed. "Why did you take human form if you hated us so much?"

"I never hated you," she said, shaking her head slowly.

Trixie muttered a long string of words. The words were familiar, so achingly familiar.

"I am . . ."

But Trixie had already turned around and left the room. The argument fizzled and stayed stale.

She fed on the bloody strips of meat savagely. She wanted to tell Trixie that she didn't mean to hurt her. She heard the door slam. Trixie had left the apartment.

The phone rang just when she was about to chase after Trixie. Nightshome at night was not a safe place. Not only would the preta appear, but murderers and thieves. Meat hunters. So much to salvage for the renderers and rags-and-bone men. The sky was already filled with dark clouds from the renders' factories, processing bodies, carcasses.

It was Ah Long. It was always Ah Long.

"Another assignment for you since the night is still young . . ."

She ignored the smooth voice, high-born and arrogant. She needed to find Trixie. She had to find Trixie.

"Payment is high. I want you to . . ."

"My partner is lost. I have to look for her," she said flatly.

"The assignment is more important. Listen, you hunt preta. You don't need human attachments. The assignment will be at another abattoir."

She growled.

"You are a beast, just like the ones you kill. You don't need human love. Go to your task. I will input the payment into your credit."

Eighteenth Hell!

The windows shattered with her scream.

A dark shape hunted the streets of Nightshome, a shadow among shadows. The skies rained ash. The steeltrains roared, metal animals with passengers in their bellies, factory workers and renderers on their own secret missions. The night food trucks waited for customers. Figures in humanaskin robes waited in their corners. In dark streets, a flick of steel, a grunt—and a new body joined the harvest. Someone would get rich tonight.

The dark shape was a beast, clawed and fanged. Having

discarded the human affectations, it was purely primal. A hunter led by smells and spoor.

Trixie.

The wolf's head sniffed the air. Blood. Bone. Marrow.

Trixie.

The claws dug into mud and broken tiles.

Tiles!

Trixie.

The beast stood up on two legs.

It held a vajira.

She found Trixie at one of the meat stalls along the river. The smell of rotting fish filled the air. And many other things too.

The stall owners scattered as the wolf shape emerged from the inky darkness. "Yao jin!" They screamed and abandoned their meat stalls in a burst of frantic action.

"Amara!" Trixie's eyes were huge. She had paused in the action of selecting a string of hearts. "Feck, I was only out for a walk!"

"This place is not safe," the wolf snapped furiously. "Come back. Please." The growl softened now, pleading, kinder.

"Amara, you are scaring everyone, including me."

She closed her skin. The dakini form went back in.

"Oh feck!" Trixie hugged her impulsively, tightly.

Szztszztszzt.

Breathing.

Preta.

Something dark and unholy grabbed Trixie from her embrace.

Trixie screamed and kicked the swirling darkness. It had multiple eyes and multiple limbs. Trixie fought like a lioness. A tendril strangled the air of her and she flopped down, limp.

"Trixie! TRIXIE!"

She crashed through walls, pursuing the darkness. She shed her jacket and ran nude. Halfway through the chase, she ignored the nudity and opened her skin.

The darkness led her on. Nightshome was a huge city, a maze with steel, factories and clusters of buildings. It moved like a black tornado, all spinning with . . .

She couldn't place the smell of it.

It was part-preta, part-something else.

But it took Trixie.

A sun burned within her chest. This must be pure rage, like the song of the universe when it came out from nothing.

Burning.

Burning.

Burning.

She ran, clawed feet, running and flying.

She was the hunter and she knew her prey was near.

She laughed and the whole universe laughed with her.

In one hand, she grabbed her vajira. In another hand, she held the skull bowl.

The skull bowl was deep with fresh crimson blood. They spilled like red tears. When they fell, they transformed into bloodstone.

Her song filled Nightshome and its citizens cried in their sleep. Yao jin, yao jin, yao jin.

She was none of those.

﷽

She pursued the darkness until it reached a renderer factory. The darkness was a sentient oil slick, flowing through the gaps and the holes, Trixie tucked within its tendrils. The chase was a game, a dance and a taunt.

"Just stop *moving*," the creature named Amara growled deep in her throat. The darkness felt more just than a simple preta, a simple hungry ghost lost between the sleeping and non-sleeping lands. More feral-intelligent, a creature like her and yet not a dakini, a protector.

The renderer factory loomed before her like a sagging drunkard, its sides run down and the paint peeling off. It reeked of human and animal ash, the aftermath of a crematorium. She knew about the renderers and vice versa. They just kept their paths clear from crossing outright. They rendered human parts down to their component bits and sold them off to the traders of the plains who then sold the minerals and metals to other traders from the satellite cities. Not much was left after Earth's death.

She savored the taste in the air. The lingering meat and oil, burnt flesh and meat. Her eyes got the heat flashes of small animals. Rodents, feeders of detritus. In the dim light, her eyes burned like three suns and their fire roared like the song of raging galaxies.

There was no sound, no human nor non-human noise. The renderers had gone home for the night. Or the factory had been abandoned not so long ago. The ash was still fresh. The flesh carts were still parked in front of the steel doors. Someone vomited there. Rancid meat and stomach acids. Congealed and half-digested meat.

Trixie.

She kicked open the doors. No subtlety there. The darkness took Trixie.

Something reverberated through the still air, a boom and a long ululation like crying or laughter. The racks of hooks rattled, touched by a passing breeze. The floor was metal, scrubbed and scuffed by multiple boots. Clusters of femurs and hip bones waited for the renderer's machine.

Amara went straight into a crouch. Her vajira screamed. Her focus narrowed. She smelled something.

"I am glad you are here, beast."

The life pod was a metal tube nestled amongst the crumbling boulders. The sky still rained fire. She reached it as the ground hissed with liquid flame.

New into the world, a protector born from fire, she tapped

the life pod with her front claws. The metal pinged. The sensation was oddly pleasurable and her bones sang with the song.

She opened it to find a woman, a young woman, curled up in a fetal position. As if she was a child about to be birthed. She was clothed in white. Her hands held a brown box. Not a skull bowl. Not a vajira. She was not a protector.

It was then the young woman opened her eyes and they were the color of clear water.

She did not scream. Instead, she uttered this word.

"Oh, feck."

They travelled a long distance before they reached the nascent Nightshome, still growing with the flood of refugees.

She took on human form, the weak limbed shape of a woman, tucking her urges in. She had black-night hair and pale skin.

"You look better," the woman said with a grin. She called herself Trixie. It was probably a bastardization of her name: Tri Xie. But she felt more like Trixie, all pink-haired and nutmeg skin. She was small for a human woman, but she moved fast. In the caravan they followed, she became the source of all healing, checking on wounds, giving advice for colds and infections. Coughs were common as abused lungs struggled to cope with the dying ash-filled air. Many developed sore eyes and one or two, bleeding pupils. Too complicated for Trixie to cope with and left to die. That was when the first few preta appeared and the creature named Amara heeded her original calling.

"You are not human," Trixie told her one night when they rested, spooning against each other's warm skin, sated with warm flesh. "I saw you in your . . . form. I don't think there were any three-eyed bipedal and blue-furred wolves running around."

Amara made a deep purring sound in her throat.

"You remind me of the Bardo. Oh, *feck*."

That was whispered in the dark, her breath a gentle warm tickle on bare skin.

"Something dark and primal—But, you've never harmed me once. That's good, isn't it?"

Then Trixie slept, stirring as her dreams disturbed her. Amara could see those dreams. Buildings falling, a child crying . . . and Trixie running running running. She had no power to stop those dreams.

Presently, her eyes focused on the figure standing before her. Male, obviously so, with musk and body fluids. He was clothed in an ironed grey shirt and starched beige pants, topped off with a long overcoat of black leather. In one gloved hand was a cane—an affectation, she realized, like her skin—and in another similarly gloved hand was a hat. His eyes were shadowed. The rest of him looked as if he were dipped in shadows.

Behind him was the darkness, curled around his figure like a protective cobra.

Behind the darkness hung Trixie, her hands tied, her legs limp. She was unconscious and unharmed.

"You."

Recognition came like a clap of thunder.

"You."

They started their agency in the third year of their stay in Nightshome. It started first as a lost-and-found and investigations agency, with Amara providing the services while Trixie did the administration and the logistics. They rented an apartment, near a relatively safer street. Steeltrains rumbled past hourly.

It paid the bills, in the form of skulls, tiny skull-shaped metal discs. It kept Amara fed. Her urges were hot in her. She was born to hunt. Red meat satisfied her and kept the urges from overwhelming her. She only let them loose when she was on a mission.

Clients ensured that they lived moderately comfortably, for Nightshome residents. Their major clients came from the renderers and the upper clans, people who wanted to keep their own dark secret urges secret. Their number-one client was Ah Long.

She hunted in flesh forests, in ruined renderer factories and along the dark streets.

"Feck, he's rich!" Trixie stared at their credit once, when Amara came back from a particularly tedious mission. She was good with counting.

Amara couldn't agree more, sucking on the chill marrow. He was arrogant, a typical rich man's son with appetites to fit his princely attitude. His voice was all she heard over the phone. She licked the blood off her lips, thinking wistfully about her skull bowl and vajira.

With the skulls they afforded her jacket and their tiny

apartment, always rumbling when one of the steeltrains thundered past.

For a while, they lived as Nighthome residents. She hunted whenever she had a mission or when clients called them in the middle of the Nightshome night.

Now, their client stood in front of her. Cocky as a man who had just rutted.

She snarled, showing her dagger fangs.

Ah Long tsked at her. The darkness slithered about him.

A revelation slammed into her.

"You are a debased dragon," she said matter-of-factly. "Cast out from nirvana."

"You are right, beast," Ah Long nodded amiably. "And you are cast out from the wheels of samsara."

"I came here, because there were things to hunt. I am a protector."

"I came here," he mocked her, "because I hunt things. Like you."

"I will bring you back to the light. Release her."

"See, you have succumbed to fleshy desires. You fell in love."

He said 'love' as if it was a pit of poison.

"Nonsense."

Where do debased dragons, their star-cores corrupted, go to? She wondered.

"Why me?" She held forth her vajira, its snarling face glittering with fangs.

"Why not? You are a dakini. I hunt dakini and feed on them."

We are both beasts, she thought, *in human form and with human affectations.*

"Release her," she said. She heard Trixie moan.

He replied by opening his skin and a dark draconic form slipped out, joining the darkness.

۞

They ignored the scourers who scourged their bodies with barbed wire, so that they could reach enlightenment or whatever they envisioned enlightenment to be. They ignored the preachers who stood at corners, waiting for skulls to trickle into their bowls shaped from human ashes.

Trixie ignored them as she shopped at the meat stalls. She bought strings of hearts for Amara. She nibbled on meat sticks. There were a few vegetables on sale. They were wilted and wan. With no sun, they couldn't grow. Mushroom growers made fortunes.

For a while, they were happy.

۞

"Release her," she repeated. She smelled rich blood. The rope had cut into Trixie's wrists and her heartsblood was flowing out.

The corrupted dragon, once a glorious celestial serpent and a controller of the seas and winds, roared with laughter. The metal racks shook with the sound. Its shadow claws crushed bones beneath them. The fall had corrupted him just as it had released her.

"Never."

She flew at the dragon, focusing her rage into an incandescent spear.

If it bleeds, I can still kill it.

The darkness met her, shielding its master from her full frontal assault. Her vajira went straight into its oily skin and cut deep.

It howled.

She howled in triumph and cut even deeper, even harder. It slashed back into her and light, her light, spilled from the wounds. The pain was more terrible than that of the preta's claws a few nights before. She howled and retaliated until the darkness writhed, its form dissipating.

"Release her," she sang and her voice was the death of a thousand stars.

"Release her," she sang and her voice was the flare of a thousand growing and dying galaxies.

"Release her."

The dragon, corrupted soul, spat black darkness back at her. She blocked it with her skull bowl and the darkness transmuted into blood, red blood, fresh blood, splashing down harmlessly onto the tiled floor. The dragon cursed and flung himself at her, claws out, hatred spikes to maim and kill.

"You cling to flesh desires, beast."

She laughed and the universe shook. "At least I am honest."

She plunged the vajira into his chest and the dragon screamed.

She ran, clawed feet, running and flying.

She was the hunter and she knew her prey was near.

She laughed and the whole universe laughed with her.

In one hand, she grabbed her vajira. In another hand, she held the skull bowl.

She supped deep of the skull bowl.

Her song filled the roiling skies.

"Amara?"

Trixie's voice was so soft as if she had long since passed into the death realm. She cradled her body and eased it down. Her wrists still bled.

Beneath her, the dragon was a twisted carcass. She had torn into him. He tasted rancid. She spat the flesh out. Let the renderers have a field day.

"Amara?" Trixie whispered. "Oh, feck, I hurt."

"I am going to get you healed," Amara promised and carried her easily down, bounding on the tiled floor on muscled legs.

"Thank you," Trixie's voice grew softer, but her heart beat strong.

They left the factory.

"Trixie," the wolf smiled and there were stars in the sky.

"Uhm?"

"Call me Soinam."

Nightshome's twilight lasted for hours, casting a weak orange glow on the flesh forests growing on its outskirts. A three-eyed wolf hunted, a dark shadow in the land of shadows. Her joyful laughter filled the forests, a song of the universe in motion.

—fin—

Lotus

Respect the waterways—anon, circa 2100.

It was the smell of burning that woke Cecily up. She got up, wrapped her sleeping robes around her body and padded out. It was still cold, even in this time of morning with the sun shining bright in the sky. She squinted—blue, with white fluffy clouds. It looked like a good day ahead. She adjusted her footing; the boat rocked gently beneath her.

"Good morning," her companion greeted her. He held a plate of burnt fish. She sighed. After all this time, he was still burning fish. And fish and fuel were not easy to obtain. Those little ikan selar—she was hit by a pang for home—came from their dwindling supplies. They needed to travel down the Waterways for the barter.

However, the fish was still salvageable, just as things were still salvageable in this day and age. She nibbled at them, grimacing at the bitter taste of carbon in her mouth. The flesh was surprisingly sweet. She used to eat them as a child, deep-fried and accompanying a special coconut rice dish her mother cooked. *On Sundays, she remembered, when every family member was home.* But where was home now?

She washed the fish down with water, savoring the taste of it. Sweet. Slightly brackish. Drinkable water was hard to come by too and every boating folk had their private stash, their hoard. So ironic that they were surrounded by water, water, water.

While she was eating, her companion—he called himself

Lent, first name Si—went back to repairing Flotsam, their boat. Flotsam was more than just a boat; he was their house, their shelter and their identity. Without Flotsam, a boater was without a name, without a solid tangible background. Yet, Flotsam had suffered from minor ills—his rotors refused to work, after a particularly long journey or his fuel tanks—ethanol, but hard to distill—were empty. He had served them faithfully, loyally.

Si whistled as he fixed the rotors. He was a trained mechanic and he loved working with machines, getting his hands dirty with engine oil and tools. Cecily watched him with a rush of tenderness in her breast. They were all travelers on the Waterways. He came from an old city called New York, she a tiny island by the name of Singapore. These places were now submerged in water—only the skyscrapers served as reminders of their joined pasts. Home, solid terra firma, was gone.

They were all using new names, even though they keenly remembered *who* they were. It was better for the Waterways where names did not matter. *New names, new places, old Earth.* They were still infants when the tsunami and subsequent melting icecaps came and conquered the land. Those who survived the Washing as they called it came out different. Changed. Transformed. And some said 'cleansed' and 'purified'. Those who lived found, salvaged and built boats. There were even large ships, the size of container ships (or were actual container vessels) serving thousands of families crammed together. They traveled the Waterways too—and trade was always good with the large ships.

Once in a while, boaters would congregate, bunched together for protection, for community. Cecily had seen one or two of these villages. Boats, big and small, bobbing with the waves.

Cooking fires sending up curls of smoke. They communicated by kayaks and by signal flares. Boater children grew nimble-footed walking on the planks joining the boats. On certain nights, the boaters would gather at one of the larger boats and tell stories about old Earth, when land was still land. Sometimes, they would sing. Sometimes, they would dance. The boating villages were always temporary. After a month or two, the boats would disperse, traveling the Waterways again.

Si cheered. He fixed the problem. Flotsam was live! She smiled, placed a straw hat on her head and prepared for another journey.

Of course, there were still patches of land here and there. They were occupied, fought over and occupied again. Many still preferred to live on the boats. Much safer, less cutthroat. The landers were vicious and territorial. Much of old Earth's history was filled with lander violence. The landers were so jealous of their land that they even forbade contact with any boater. Ironically, some of the small lander communities still depended on the boaters for essential items like food and clean water.

Flotsam moved forward, Si at the wheel now. Cecily made an offering to Maju, the Goddess of the sea, and then stood beside her companion. It would be a long day.

⁂

"Land ho!" What a misnomer!—A common boaters' saying.

It was not long before they sighted the familiar broken jagged outline of former skyscrapers. Si was suddenly quiet. They seemed to have traveled back to his old home. As Flotsam approached the place where an impressive Statue once stood, he turned sharply to Cecily and said, "Let's make it a short visit. There are many better places to go to."

Cecily wondered about his abrupt change in mood. And "places". What an odd word to use. But she kept her peace and took over the wheel, watching the former buildings, now frameworks of steel and concrete, come closer. It was a sober yet beautiful sight. There were still people occupying the more stable buildings. They welcomed the arrival of the boaters, because they brought much needed barter and gossip.

A hush fell upon both of them as Flotsam slid between former roads, his rotors chopping noisily. The sounds echoed around them, like a steel canyon. Flights of birds, disturbed by Flotsam's noisy presence, took flight, their squawks echoing. Cecily could see nets, very fine nets, erected across certain areas, no doubt to net unsuspecting birds. She had fried sparrow before. Goddess knows what kinds of birds were being cooked here.

As it was getting late, they dropped anchor next to a building with a "School" sign swinging crookedly from it. In the slight breeze, the sign made soft rattling sounds. They cooked a small dinner—again with fish and some flatbread made a couple of days earlier—and went back to bed, making passionate love before falling asleep.

Cecily dreamed. She knew she dreamed because she was back at her grandmother's. There were pictures, photographs and memorabilia hung on the walls. The ancestral altar had lit candles on it.

It was the 15th lunar day of the month, for there were fresh lotus blooms—fist-sized pink buds—in the simple porcelain vase.

Her grandmother and her mother were folding paper money into ingots and they were chatting about daily matters. Someone in the family had given birth to a daughter. A relative from so-and-so was getting married. Simple things. Normal things.

Then her grandmother, dressed in a plain light blue kebaya, lifted up her head and beckoned to Cecily who felt as if she was standing in a corner, like some ghost. It was odd, because her grandmother and her mother were now ghosts, people from her past.

"Ci Ci, never forget who you are. Remember your roots, just as the lotus roots dig deep into the soil," her grandmother said, with a gentle smile in her lips and eyes.

Suddenly, inexplicably, as dreams are, Cecily was showered in petals. Pink lotus petals.

⁂

The next morning saw them sailing down boulevards of water. They did some trade with some of the folk living in the buildings. From the tenants (as they called themselves now) came the supplies of water and some vegetables, grown indoors. From Cecily went soft wool shawls, comfortable for chilly mornings. The temperature never seemed to have warmed up ever since. After the trade and some light-hearted gossip, they bade farewell to the tenants and moved on.

Cecily took the wheel again. She felt at ease with the steering of Flotsam. It felt intuitive. As she steered, her mind eased into a semi-meditative state. She went back to the dream and wondered deeply. She was indeed surprised to see her grandmother and her mother in a dream. They had not appeared to her for a while. She pondered on the images.

Afternoon whispered in a brief downpour, forcing them to drop anchor again. This time, it was an abandoned hotel. Si decided to give Flotsam a once-over again while Cecily moved lower deck to do some knitting. She was recently given a basketful of homespun yarn by a woman who lived alone on a small sailing boat. She wanted to make good use of the yarn.

Yet something nudged at her. A soft inner voice or some stray thought. She put down her darning needles and wore her poncho (again, from the woman who gave her the yarn).

"I am going to explore the hotel," she announced to an astonished Si who stared at her with worry in his grey eyes.

"There might be unsavory tenants hanging around," he protested as she donned her gumboots. "You know how dangerous this part of the Waterways can be. You know, ghettos and the like."

"You are still stuck in old-Earth thinking," Cecily chided him gently. Si could be so sensitive sometimes. She brought along her wooden waster, shaped like a medieval longsword. She had salvaged this a few months ago, straight out from an old store selling military ware.

Si looked at her. "I am just concerned, that's all. You a petite woman and all . . . "

She laughed. "I have this!" She waved the wooden longsword. "And I know how to use it." *Petite woman?* She chuckled and caught sight of her reflection in one of the cupboards. *Dark hair, dark eyes, swarthy skin bathed by constant sun.* Old-Earth thinking, indeed!

Cecily stepped off the boat and through an open window.

People are so anal-retentive about the concept of wealth. What is wealth? Money? Riches? Resources?—an excerpt from a neo-Marxist chapbook, circa 2040.

She stepped into a dark world.

A dark and dank world, filled with broken beams, broken window shards and broken furniture. Musty curtains still hung from window frames, torn and frayed. Some had been removed, obviously by inventive tenants. She looked around cautiously for any sign of tenant activity. So far, only silence or a silence laced with the sounds of animals roosting somewhere and of water dripping somewhere.

Water. Her ears perked up and she walked on, using her waster to push away debris. She seemed to be in the mezzanine area of the hotel. It was once grand, this hotel. It was now a hollow husk with a skeletal metal frame and fallen beams. She found a baby grand, still intact, the keys yellowed and the cover mildewed. She played a simple tune—it was rusty and the song vibrated around her. It was a familiar tune and she hummed softly to herself. Then she left the baby grand and headed towards the direction of the dripping water.

The hotel had sagged in the middle, much like a failed soufflé. She found her footing gradually, precariously and walked, sometimes crawled on all fours, on the ripe carpeting. It was vivid red velvet once.

Just then the world around her plunged. Concaved sharply. She grabbed onto some protruding beams, swung herself onto a ledge—

—and gazed right into a large pool of emerald water.

Sunlight had lanced in from the top half of the building, illuminating the pool of water and a field of . . . lotus flowers and leaves.

This time she gawked, just gawked, because the lotus flowers were as big as dinner plates and the leaves were huge, circular. The petals glowed, taking her breath away. There was movement in the water, concentric ripples ever widening and criss-crossing; she spied shapes swimming lazily beneath the surface. *Fish.* By the look of it, large carp or koi.

She sat down, overwhelmed. She remembered her dream. She also remembered that all parts of the lotus could be used. And the fish. Fresh food. Nelumbo nucifera. Cyprinus carpio. And the pool was *huge*, by the looks of it, ballroom-size and probably larger.

There was wealth in front of her. She reached out, dipped her right hand into the water and scooped out a handful of the cool-warm liquid. Tasted it and gasped with instant pleasure—it was drinkable water!

Wealth.

She flung a worried look upwards. There were no tenants around. The hotel was empty. This pool of water with its wealth was hers.

With some ingenuity, she knew, she could harvest the lotus

leaves and roots. The roots could be used for stews, soups and pickles. Even eaten slightly raw, with crisp sweetness. The leaves could be used to wrap rice. The flowers could yield seeds, also delicious roasted or grounded flour. The fish could be caught, salted or fried. So many possibilities, so many . . .

And the water. *Drinkable.* And when treated, definitely usable for so many things. She felt giddy with joy. *No more barter, no more hoarding. No more worrying.*

She emerged hurriedly out into the open and clambered back into the boat. Si stood up from the small oven; he was preparing a late lunch. She smelled frying fish and bread. She told herself that they were going to eat much better food now.

"Si!" She called out and he came up to her, his face filled with relief. "You will never believe what I have found . . . "

"Unsavory tenants?" He teased her, smiling to take the sting out of his words.

"No. Much better."

She brought him through the hotel window, led him down the dark path leading to the pool of lotus flowers and leaves. He stood stock still, eyes open wide, taking in the sight. *Drinking* it in.

"This is wealth in front of us, Si!" Cecily said excitedly. "And drink the water. It is definitely drinkable water."

He did so and his face lit up with elation, like a child eating candy for the first time. "Unbelievable. Perhaps, this place is being fed by some unknown natural source." He sipped the water again. "Sweet. So sweet."

They both watched the lotus flowers glowing quietly in the sunlight and marveled at the fish flitting through the lotus stems submerged in the water. They held hands, feeling as though they were Adam and Eve, in an abundant Garden of Eden.

Later, they brought in nets and caught two large carp, obviously well-fed by the nutrients in the pool and heavy with much flesh and milt. Cecily collected a handful of lotus roots, covered in rich dark mud. They had a hearty meal that night, of lotus soup and baked fish. They kept the leftovers in the supply box and went to bed with full stomachs.

۞

They stayed next to the hotel for a few more days, guarding their treasure. Cecily was secretly well pleased that there had been no other claimants to the wealth. They found it. It was *theirs*. Si, ever the mechanic and the scientist, attempted to look for the source of the water but to no avail. It was a mystery and Cecily was glad that it should stay a mystery. *Imagine what would happen if people started finding the source and wars would break out,* she thought darkly.

Cecily harvested some of the large plate-like leaves and wrapped rice with them. The rice came out lightly perfumed and fragrant. Eaten with the fat fish flesh, it was heavenly.

Si created a makeshift mobile of sorts, hung with dangly shiny and noisy implements (metal cans, forks and spoons) to act as an alarm. If anyone—tenant or otherwise—triggered it, they would know that the pool of lotus flowers had been compromised. Invaded.

It was theirs and Cecily was determined to keep it that way. It was hard to come by natural sources of food—and so much wealth as well. They both knew sustainable farming, having spent years cultivating their own gardens; they would make sure that the water, the lotuses and the fish remained a permanent fixture.

Cecily had never felt so contented before. Granted that traveling down the Waterways, with its diverse pathways, gave her some satisfaction but this . . . this wealth was so heartening to the spirit.

She started to nurse thoughts of remaining in the old city, right beside her hotel and its wealth. Not as a tenant per se, but living in their boat and using the wealth. Protecting it from harm's way. She started having fantasies of having children and having them grow up with the lotuses and fish.

It was immensely heartening.

Live free—an old saying, circa old-Earth period.

She found herself dreaming about her grandmother. Dressed in elegant kebaya with richly embroidered goldfish and a forest-green sarong, she was cooking something in the kitchen. Even in the dream, it smelled gorgeous and the dream-Cecily experienced a strange thing: her mouth watered, at the smell of the cooking. It must be a festival day in the dream because there were plates of festive food on the kitchen counter. And sweetmeats and multi-colored kueh on platters, mind boggling diverse in variety.

There was laughter coming from the living room and Cecily walked towards the sound. What she saw confused her.

People whom she had met as a traveler of the Waterways were congregating in the living room. Some sat on the sofa. Some lounged on the floor. Everyone was at ease and laughing. There was the woman whom she had traded the yarn with. There were the tenants whom she and Si had met earlier and exchanged gossip, water and vegetables. Some of the people were less familiar but certainly encountered. A family of six—South Indians—chatted animatedly with the yarn woman; she remembered they gave her spices and gave her recipes in exchange for clean water. A single dusky-skinned man with a day's growth of beard massaged another man's back—she had met them at one of the great trading posts. They were big ship dwellers and were lovers. They taught her how to weave a certain kind of scarf and she gave them two large balls of orange-colored yarn. Even Si was there, chuckling away. He looked much younger, less care-worn. Even handsome.

"Dinner's ready!" Her grandmother's voice startled her and there was soft chatter as all the visitors moved towards the large dining table. There were bowls and containers of food and desserts.

There were also curried fish that looked suspiciously like fat carp and bundles of rice (wrapped in lotus leaf). The scents were intoxicating.

"Come, eat, share." Her grandmother was saying. Cecily watched as the visitors, including Si, approached the table and placed their own contributions on the table. Pakkora. Irish stew. Vegetarian minestrone. Fry bread. Even Si's burnt fish. And everyone ate from the various dishes, their faces happy.

Someone tugged at her arm. She looked around and saw a little Eurasian girl, about four to five. She had Si's eyes and tanned skin. "Mother," the little girl lisped but her words were clear and her eyes bright. "Share."

She woke up then and stared at the roof of the lower deck. Si was snoring softly next to her. She placed a hand on her flat abdomen, realization dawning.

They managed to harvest more of the lotus roots and bottled the water for further consumption. Their upper deck was laden with food and water. Enough to last a month or even more. Si rigged up the distiller to clean the water and Cecily washed the mud off the roots.

The mobile jangled, breaking the comfortable silence. It was a sharp rude sound shattering a peaceful morning. Si got to his feet and ran to confront the intruder.

A tenant—an old man, hobbled with age, dressed in plain yellow shirt and tattered brown pants—looked up shocked, with eyes wide as if he was caught in the middle of searchlights. His arms held a bundle of lotus flowers and one large fish dangled from his right arm.

"Thief!" Si snarled and leapt over, knocking the man down with a solid punch on the jaw. The lotus flowers fell, scattered. The fish flopped on the unsteady floor, still living, mouth gaping away. It was that fresh. There was a feral look in Si's face, an unwholesome gleam in his eyes. Hunter's eyes. Predator's eyes. "Thief!" And he landed a blow on the old man's face again.

The old man cowered, trembling and terrified. His face was bruised. His limbs shook.

"Sorry, sir, I was just taking some of the 'looms and 'ish," the old man quavered. He must have been in his late seventies. "It is all out there, free, sir . . ."

"We found it, old man," Si snapped. Cecily realized how *ugly* he looked like that. What had happened to her quiet and placid companion? "Now, go."

"But sir, I have 'randchildren to feed and my youngest daughter is 'regnant," the old man choked and wept. Cecily's heart clenched.

"It's ours," Si bit out, his eyes dark with rage.

Cecily knelt down, picked the fish up and gave it to the old man. "Here, take it. You need it." The fish was slick and warm, still twitching, in her hands.

The old man looked at her half-fearfully, half-thankfully. Grabbed the fish and scrambled back onto a little run-down kayak. He pedaled away as if he was being chased by a ferocious demon.

"Why did you hit him?" Cecily shot accusing eyes at Si. "He was just an old man."

"He was taking our food," Si answered grimly, color still high in his face.

Mine. Ours. Theirs.

There was a horrible taste in her mouth. It was bile.

It was disgust.

She refused to talk to her companion for the rest of the day, spending more time below deck. She was unable to knit; her thoughts were heavy and sobering. She kept on rewinding the incident in her head: the old man, the old man hit on the face, Si punching him, the lotuses and fish flung onto the floor.

She placed a palm on her belly. She knew that she was pregnant. The more so they needed the pool of lotus flowers and fish. For the nutrients and the protein. For . . .

The old man quivering with fear, balled up in a fetal position, as Si punched him.

Mine. Ours. Theirs.

There was the taste of bitter bile again in her mouth and she washed it down with clean water.

It was theirs. She wanted to believe that. They found it. However, there were people who needed the water, the lotuses and the fish as well. The pool was theirs too.

Were they indeed living free? Or were they still tied up in old feuds and conflicts driven by need? Should they stake a claim on the lotus pond? Was she turning into a lander?

Her head throbbed. She felt sick to the core.

She spent a sleepless dreamless night and woke up, feeling exhausted. Si was up early and making breakfast. She could smell a sweet fragrance: they had grounded the lotus seeds into flour and he was making pancakes from it.

She ate in silence just as Si ate in silence. They were both mulling over the same incident.

"I don't like the way you hit the old man," she began by saying and Si looked at her closely. "He needed the food for his family."

Si swallowed his pancake hard and stared at her. "I just don't like the idea of him taking from the pool."

"The pool is wild. The lotuses and fish are wild. It is a free place, Si." Cecily started to feel angry and knew that her voice was becoming louder. "The water flows free."

"Now you are talking," Si whined, his face sullen. "Just a couple of days ago, you wanted the pool to yourself."

Cecily shut her mouth. The words struck home. *It hurt.* She did want the pool. It felt like hers. It was hers. Or was it?

"I think we should go," she managed to say again, her voice soft. "Take what we need and go. The Waterways will provide for us, I am sure." *And I am pregnant—*

Si's eyes. They were angry/sad/disappointed. "Why? Why should we go? I am tired of being a boater and this place is just perfect."

"If we stay," Cecily said firmly now. "There will be disagreements. Quarrels. Fights." She sipped the water. "If we stay, the pool will not be free anyway. It will come with a price. Our price. Their price. We will end up paying."

"Feh," Si spat and stalked out from the upper deck, throwing the half-eaten pancake petulantly onto the floor. It crumbled instantly. Cecily could only stare and feel a dull ache in her heart. Conflict, unpleasant and dangerous, was already starting to creep in like winter chill.

She went to the pool and sat down next to it, beside the musty beams and steel rafters. Sunlight still glowed in the middle. Fish swam peacefully. The lotus flowers tilted their faces towards the sun. It was such an idyllic place. And it could so easily become a place of tension, anger and—

Boaters lived free. It was a code all of them knew, understood and took to heart. With the Washing, the concept of home was removed and the Waterways were created, because Earth was now covered with water. They had taken away the concept of money; barter trade was the lingua franca now. Boaters moved freely. Fluidly. Nobody made rules for them.

Staying next to the hotel, guarding the pool, had begun to engender unspoken rules. If they stayed longer, she was sure that they would start making laws. *When to harvest the lotus plants. How many to harvest? How many fishes to be netted? How many liters of waters to be collected?* And definitely the penalties would be implemented, if such laws were being transgressed, breached. They would end up behaving no better than the landers. *Perhaps, we are no better than the landers, because we are all humans,* Cecily pondered, concluding her internal argument with this sad realization.

She buried her face in her hands. She had begun to love this pool and its riches. Yet deep down inside her, she knew that the pool was *free.* The lotus plants were wild and so were the fish. The water was free to everyone who used it. If she stayed, she would put a price on all of them.

The pool was to be shared.

She clambered back up to the boat, only to find Si sitting contemplatively on the upper deck of Flotsam. He had somehow cleared the pancake off the floor.

"Cecily," Si said and his voice was gentle. He came over and held her hands. "I am sorry. I was behaving like a royal jerk."

They hugged each other tightly. When they let go, Si gazed at her. "I have thought it over. We should go. I mean, there are paths in the Waterways least traveled. And I am getting tired of New York anyway." He smiled, trying to lighten the mood. "Never liked the city . . . Makes me mad all the time."

"Si!" She said. "Oh, Si."

They both made their last trip to the pool and harvested whatever they needed. They bottled enough water to last until the next Trading Post, netted enough fish to be salted and frozen; and bundled enough lotus plants—flowers, roots and leaves—for a month. Enough for personal consumption and for barter. When they looked back, there were still many lotus plants left, swaying slightly in the breeze. The fish were still plentiful. The water was still sweet to the taste. The pool was wild and free.

Cecily packed everything in the supply box while Si lifted anchor and started the engines. Flotsam sputtered into life once more, sounding as if he was grumbling about the previous inertia.

With not a backward glance, they sailed away and journeyed down the Waterways once more.

—fin—

A Sky Full of Swiftlets

When I was a child, the sky was full of swiftlets. I would wake up before dawn and wait for them. In between the liminal time of dawn and early morning, they would arrive, a flock of tiny dark shapes darting about in their own language of flight. I would watch them, wishing that they would stop flying, because they were so fast, so swift.

Yet when I grew older, all I wanted was to see the swiftlets fly. That was when the Two-Headed came and turned my home into burning fields. That was the time when the sky was empty.

The Two-Headed were vile beasts who came in their shining ships, wielding their energy weapons. They bore the heads of Terran equines, hideous abominations with red eyes and sharp teeth. They plundered my home and forced us into hiding. I was young then, no more than eleven.

Jadeen taught me archery. We did not have energy weapons. We had seen the damage wrought upon human flesh. We fought back the way our ancestors had.

The Hiders attacked the Two-Headed in hit-and-run raids, destroying their camps, stealing their food, because they were consuming ours.

I was angry and I grew more so when I turned fourteen.

I cut my mane off on the Day of Light Winds, our New Year. It was a significant day. The harvest was done and the sun was warm, inviting. The fields would shimmer with the ripening gold saleet, the grain my home was known for. It was the day when the grandmothers would pound the grain into flour, before making the grilled buns filled with meat and chopped river chives.

It was the traditional day of plenty. Everyone looked forward to it. I cut my mane, telling myself that it was my own rite of passage . . .

The surviving families had retreated into the nashot cliffs, tunneling into the myriad caves. Swiftlets used to live in these caves, building their delicate bowl-shaped nests on the inner cave walls. Now they were gone, the caves bereft of their fluttering wings and high-pitched chirps. Where the swiftlets used to fly rose tiny fireplaces, surrounded by huddled groups of men, women and children. We had all grown used to the layers of guano and the rippling sea of insects feeding on the dead and dying. Children had learnt how to cover their noses, ears and mouths when they slept.

Looking at my family and friends fueled an anger within me. They should not be suffering like this! I stalked out of the cliffs, into the humid night, bow in my claws . . .

The night wind brought the scents to my nose. The sula trees so alive with amber sap. The vines of glow-blooms lighting the night path. Somewhere, a clear stream cut through the forest: sweet sweet aqua. We were the descendents of Terran colonists, but our bodies had evolved.

I smelled a rank disturbing scent, like rotting algae ponds: The Two-Headed.

My nose wrinkled. I licked my upper canines. They had not grown sharp yet. I had not come of age. My rite of passage was not over.

I crept purposefully forward, my nightwalk now a hunt. My

feetpads moved quietly on the forest loam, feeling it warm and awake through the sensitive skin. There was a band of Two-Headed roving about. They were inching towards the nashot cliffs.

I got down on my knees, crawling. A part of me wanted to alert Jadeen, my father and the uncles. Or rally the grandmothers. For a moment I was afraid.

Their guttural snorts informed me that I was close. They were pacing in front of one of the least explored cliffs. The smell of guano was overwhelming. Their equine faces grimaced, showing their unnatural teeth. "Horses do not have sharp teeth," one of the old grandmothers had told me. She was the Storykeeper, protecting our histories. Except that the Two-Headed were not horses.

They were beasts.

They stepped into a cave, their talons holding black cylinders, their energy weapons. I bared my teeth, my skin-hair bristling. I drew an arrow and nocked it, preparing to fire when ready. My heart thumped against my chest, vibrating against my ribcage.

Noises echoed around me. The cave had an unusually wide chamber with a soaring roof. My feet sank into a thick sludge of guano and I almost growled aloud in annoyance. The band of Two-Headed was in front of me, unaware of my presence.

There was a soft distinctive chirp. Like a whistle.

Another chirp answered it.

I stood stock-still, listening in disbelief. That chirp. That song. Could it be?

Slowly, half-awed, I looked up, seeing the tell-tale signs of nests. A couple of fleet dark shapes flew in the dim interior. Shadows moving in shadows.

My heart beat harder now. Swiftlets!

The fury within me solidified into hard red-hot steel. I fired the arrow. There was an unearthly howl, amplified by the cave chamber, and the sizzle of energy weapons being activated.

I ran.

⁂

"That was a stupid thing to do, Bei," Jadeen snarled at me, his eyes bright with anger and worry. "Shooting in the dark like that. You could have gotten yourself killed!"

My father glared at me too. The womenfolk clustered nearby, wrapped in their patterned shawls, their eyes shining in the darkness.

"I am sorry," I said, shaking my head vigorously, the short mane rustling against my nape. "But I saw something. Something important. The swiftlets are back!"

Jadeen's aged face lit up for a moment, before crumbling in on itself like brittle clay. "No. Impossible. They disappeared twelve circles ago."

"It is true, Jadeen. I heard them."

Whispers. The women talked among themselves, some of them pulling their shawls tighter, as if chilled.

"They disappeared. I saw the last nests burned," Jadeen repeated, his tone strict. I stifled down a desire to yell at him to listen, to listen to me.

"I heard them, Jadeen. They are in the unexplored part of the nashot caves." My claws balled into fists.

Jadeen looked at me levelly. He sighed deeply, slapping his hands on his thighs. He suddenly appeared older, more weary.

"Take us there, Bei."

We headed towards the cliffs when we knew that the Two-Headed were not active. They were often inactive during the day. The sun seemed to hurt them. Jadeen was the first to enter the cave, followed by my father and the rest of the men folk. I gripped my bow in my hand, smelling the guano and listening for the telltale chirp.

Second Uncle lifted the gas-light up and it illuminated the entire chamber. The light flared, soaring up the cliff walls like a live flame. We followed the light, seeing the palm-sized nests woven from the spittle of swiftlets, clinging to the walls in the shape of crescent moons. I could see the wonder in everyone, the sparkle in their eyes. Silence. Amazement.

Jadeen picked an abandoned nest from the cave floor, examining it in his hand. "Tien!" He used the word for amazement. "Tien!"

"Now do you believe me?" I said, catching glimpses of tiny darting shapes above our heads.

Before Jadeen could answer, the sky collapsed.

The Two-Headed attack was unexpected. They used roaring bombs, crumbling the cliff walls.

The menfolk yelled their battle cries, launching themselves into combat. I shuddered, my bow before me, the arrow nocked. My hands shook. I wanted so much to fight. Protecting the swiftlets had become my passion, my own personal fight, but I was afraid.

Two-Headed soldiers fired their energy weapons. My loved ones were falling around me. I saw Jadeen mouthing something as he fell, a gaping wound on his left side. My uncles were trampled under cruel talons. They were bleeding from their mouths, choking in their own fluids. Yet they fought back, stabbing with their knives. Father battled a black-furred Two-Headed, slashing red gouges into its barrel chest with his nif dagger. Even in the heat of the battle, I found myself shocked that the Two-Headed bled red, just like us.

I must have shouted something. All I knew was my rage, bubbling up like the hot springs in the valley, incandescent and burning. Images passed before my eyes: my mother and the grandmothers making the grilled buns for the Day of Light Winds, their nimble fingers knitting the buns together; Jadeen teaching me how to hold the bow correctly; the saleet fields lush with life and hope; and the swiftlets dancing in the sky.

My nif dagger was in my hand. A red haze covered my vision. I tasted blood. Hot, metallic, edged with an odd sourness.

I stared into two pairs of crimson eyes and two large open maws with jagged teeth. My claws were smeared with fresh blood, tightly clenched around the hilt of my dagger. The blade was buried deep in a Two-Headed's chest.

With a guttural curse, I grounded the dagger deeper. The Two-Headed buckled, trying to throw me off. I could hear its labored breathing. I bared my fangs.

The Two-Headed's mouths bled. Dark red blood, now coating my arms. I kicked my feet into its gut. I wanted it to die.

A violent spasm threw me backwards and I found myself flung away. The Two-Headed staggered towards me, my hilt jutting out from its chest. It was dying now, but its eyes still burned with hate.

I sobbed. My ribs felt as if they were broken into pieces. The last thing I saw was the Two-Headed reaching towards me.

***

"Shh," said a feminine voice—Ma?—and I felt a gentle caress on my cheeks. I opened my eyes to see my aunt leaning over. "Drink this." The edge of a bowl touched my lips and I sipped greedily, tasting the familiar bitterness of herbs.

I winced. My sides were terribly sore now, neatly bandaged up and held into place with a binding band.

"Where … Ma?" I spoke like a little girl and I hated it, even though I was weak and wobbly like a kid. I was fourteen, about to turn fifteen. I was growing up.

"She is with your father and Jadeen," my aunt smiled sadly. "They are hurt badly, but they will live. We are strong people, Bei." She squeezed my hand. "Strong people."

She gathered her shawl and the half-finished bowl of herbal brew, moving away to tend to other injured. I saw my uncles, similarly bandaged, delirious with pain.

The women sang in the night, their voices reedy but sincere. Their song was of the swiftlets, silent and brave in the morning light. I listened, sobbing into my blankets.

Despite my mother's and aunt's stern reprimands, I managed to shuffle my way to the nashot cave. The week-old smell of the Two-Headed lingered in the air like rotten eggs. I let my senses guide my way. The cave beetles and insects had removed any traces of the skirmish, yet an echo of anger remained. I could feel it on my skin.

Sunlight was streaming down from cracks in the natural ceiling, bathing the chamber in gold. I raised my arms up, feeling the warmth. Yes, the nests were there. A few of them, not the hundreds of old, but they were there. I could hear them now. Their chirps. Their songs.

Something startled the swiftlets and they began to dart about in a mass of black wings and black bodies.

For a moment, the chamber was nothing but a swirling cloud of swiftlets. I drank in the sight, remembering it so that I could tell my children if I lived that long.

"Bei."

I turned around to see my teacher. "Jadeen."

His eyes were fixed on the swiftlets, full of wonder. "This is amazing."

"Yes."

We watched the swiftlets in silence. The alarm over, they slowly settled and returned to their crescent-shaped nests.

"Bei, we have decided," Jadeen said, hesitation in his voice. "We are moving."

A splash of cold shock hit me, followed by indescribable fury. "No!"

"We have to. The Two-Headed know where we are."

"No! What about the swiftlets? Do they not need protection too?"

"Bei, the village needs our protection. Think about the women, the children."

"No! What about our memories of the swiftlets? Do you want our children and their children to forget about the swiftlets?"

I must have crossed a line. In my state I dared to cross many. A claw swiped across my cheek. Jadeen glared at me. "We have no choice, Bei."

"We have a choice. We can choose to fight back!"

"No."

I lifted a trembling hand and touched my stinging cheek, both ashamed and angry. I watched Jadeen walk away, limping from his injuries, and I watched my childhood leave with him.

So I did what I could.

I cut my mane off on the Day of Light Winds. While the women made the grilled buns and the village prepared to celebrate, I threw my mane into the wind and made my way alone into the wilderness.

I had grown up, I told myself, the wind cold against my exposed scalp. I sucked in a lungful of air, trying to feel brave.

The swiftlets would fly in the sky again.

I ran up the small mound, nif dagger in my hand. I could hear them. I could smell them. Two-Headed warriors. I hefted the dagger, testing its weight, feeling reassured, comforted. It was a gift from Father, blessed by Jadeen my mentor. It had tasted blood. It would taste blood again.

Revulsion, red-hot, foul like vomit, clenched my stomach. Two-Headed confounded me. Heads of horses and not one, but two on a body—how could they even think? But they did, after some obscure fashion.

I was now sixteen. My mane had been shorn and remained shorn as my personal promise. I had come of age, my upper canines sharpened. If I had stayed at the village, I would have a new name to mark my adulthood. I would also have a feast held in my honor. I was a Hider, but I would not hide anymore. I was Bei. I had been Bei.

I was now Nashot.

Swiftlet Caves. Swiftlets.

Now it was my new self, my new name, my new identity. I fought for them.

I fought for myself.

Day of plenty

Listen to ahma making the buns

Listen to her sing.

Watch the saleet gold in the sunrise.

I am home, ahma.

I am home, ahda.

I am home.

With a growl rattling from my throat glands, I stalked my prey. May I be as swift as the ones who dwelled in the caves.

—fin—

The Lessons of the Moon

1. Sea of Rains
Waxing, waning, dark moon, crescent, full –
like rain that comes and drench
the desert of my being
water
the bare sand, caress the skin, grow seeds.

2. Sea of Crises
Blame the fullness for the insanity that comes
like the crack of lighting or the giggle
of a child at the sight of buffoons
balloons
staying afloat at the sky,
subject to the whim of the wind.

3. Sea of Tranquillity
I hope to remain calm –
consistent, sure as the tides
and as violent as rip currents that pull me
apart,
tear me inside out,
outside in.

4. *Landing*
Landing, hoping to land,
that's all I want, all I desire –
Landing.
I have been storm-tossed, thrown away, pulled apart:
terra firma, solid ground.
Land now, just land.

I am staring out of the window, at the colors that sweep across the sky, the pinks and the oranges and the red and the rare streak of purple. They cover me, the patches on my chest going up and down. I am awash with colors, swimming in them. I am alive.

My IV drip feeds me, giving me the salt and glucose. My mouth craves the feel and texture of food. Oranges. Apples. A fat juicy medium-rare steak so red that the blood blends with the caramelized onion sauce. Glasses of wine, water and fruit smoothies. Quivering red jellies gleaming like pure ruby, tasting of fine plum and grape liquor. Food, glorious food. Hard to eat when your tastebuds hate you and your intestines reject food straight away.

They are saying that I am changing. Like the moon. I am so low in energy now, the dark moon, that I can only lie on my bed and stare at the colors. Sometimes, I am in my waxing phase, energy coming back—and when I am full, I can do so many things. I write. I dance. I cook. I move. My garden of green and red chilli, of rosemary and mint. Then I crash and I am back to square one.

My limbs feel like weights. My joints ache and my pain synapses are on fire. I am brought back to earth. I am changing. Into what form, I am not sure.

I am not changing into a phoenix, for sure. The thing running in me isn't some mythical bird due for re-birth. The thing inside me is some insidious beast, sometimes tame, sometimes vicious. All I can do is to chain it down.

Now I am earthbound.

They want me in a Pod, so that I can live further and enjoy more years. I am not sure I want to fly a Pod and fight bad aliens in space, where physics still works and there is no sound. If my body fails, the surgeon tries to reassure me, be patient, this disease needs patience, I will have a new body and I will be a warrior. A good cause. I am fighting for something noble.

Am I?

How many warriors are there out fighting? Are they stationed next to the moon? Can I be the moon instead?

I want to be the moon?

When I die, eventually, I want to be buried in the Sea of Tranquillity, or have my ashes scattered. Pods get destroyed at the end. I do not think Pod warriors retire. I want to be scattered like stars. Turn into diamonds. Better than just being destroyed in a burst of mangled steel and voiceless pain.

My little girl visits me during visiting hours. She has just turned five. But somehow, she knows what I am going through. She looks at me with huge dark eyes. I don't know how I look like. I don't want to know. I refuse having a mirror in the room. The nurses laugh and say I look beautiful. I think they are just pulling my leg and lying through their immaculate teeth. The kind of polite laughter able-bodied and healthy people use, the tone they take with me. "Hang on in there", "You will be fine", "You should pull your bootstraps", nonsense nonsense more nonsense. Where are you when I am in pain? Where are you when I need help?

My little girl is unafraid, daring. She is always like that. She will pick the coat's button daisies growing outside our house and braid them into tiny bracelets. Coat's button daisies have smiley faces and grow wild everywhere. Endemic. Pest. Resilient. I think they are more resilient than me. I love them. When I sleep, the bracelets are beside me. There is sap and sweetness in my nose. When I wake, the nurses have removed them away. Thrown them into the bin. For fear of contamination, they explain. This is a germ-free environment.

There will always be new bracelets.
They remind that I am resilient. I hang on.
I am hanging on.

"Remember the dandelions?" My little girl would whisper next to my ear. "Remember the dandelions, will you? Please? There are no dandelions in space."

I remember them. They are not really dandelions, but they have similar blowballs. I used to pick her up after day care, plucking the flowers and blowing at the cotton-like puff. She loved the seeds floating in the air. I told her about the pappus that act like parachutes, drifting in the wind. She loves these memories.

'Yes," I reply and my voice rattles in my lungs. My pain synapses snap and bite. My body is rebelling against me.

"You will be in a Pod," she would say later. "You will be like the pappus. You will fly away. I will miss you."

"Yes," I say and I think about the moon. Always the moon.

☽☽☾

Waxing, waning, dark moon, crescent, full –
like rain that comes and drench
the desert of my being
water
the bare sand, caress the skin, grow seeds.

☽☽☾

The Pod is big, like a silver egg with wings and turrets built in. A mobile missile, piloted and inhabited by a brain. My brains. Someone else's brains. Brains, without bodies. A mess of synapses and nerve, stuck in a machine.

I see the Pod in images they show me, just to convince me how fabulous it is. I am on a noble mission. To fight for the Earth in an egg. To fight for humanity against big bad aliens who want to conquer us and our planet.

To fight for my family.

"I want my ashes scattered in the Sea of Tranquility," I state calmly to the attending surgeon. "I want my dust to mingle with the moon dust."

Smiling, he scribbles something down on his writing pad.

How quaint. He wants to humor me. We fly through space to fight aliens and he is writing on paper. Like me, some parts of him have not changed. We remain changed and unchanged. Like the moon.

Some people are afraid of change.
I am changing.
I should not be afraid of change.

So, when they fit me into the Pod, I am ready. My little girl cries and kisses my cheek wetly. Her arms hang onto me. She refuses to let go. "Mama, mama!"

"Make bracelets for me," I whisper. "Wo ai ni." I love you. "Go to your mummy." I mean my wife. She will miss me too. I miss her butterfly kisses. "Wo ai ni," I repeat. "Listen to your mummy." My little girl smiles through her tears.

My wife stands beside my little girl, her eyes dry. She has accepted. She is still accepting. She is tired. She is now free. She kneels down and holds my hand, rests her cheek against mine. I have known her for fourteen years. She is beautiful. She will always be beautiful. She has been there when my synapses flare up and I burn inside out. She has been there when I collapsed in my chair and felt like shit. She has fed me herbal soups and told me stories about her family. I have pulled her back. She is earthbound, because of me. Now she is free. I have given back her wings.

She begins to cry now, her tears streaming down her face. My heart clenches painfully and I cry too. My little girl is quickly coaxed away from the bed by one of the nurses. I hear her sobbing outside the room. "Mama, mama, MAMA!"

"Shh, don't," I soothe my wife, patting her hand with my fingers. My fingers look bony, my skin so dry, so thin. "Please don't cry."

"Remember me," she sobs. "When you are with the stars."

"I will," I whisper.

I am going to be free.

I am going to fly.

The doctors and technicians shoo my wife away. I see her behind the glass, blurred, separated from me. Like she is under water. My little girl is not there. Is she spared from this unkindness?

Then, the metal synapses and cords snap into me. I feel a brief pain, like fire in my nerves, in my joints. When I finally open my eyes, I am in the Pod. My human flesh body is gone.

I am going to fly.

I learn and unlearn to love my new body. The Pod. It is all metal, motherboard and circuits that form my new blood vessels. My new synapses. There is no body, no flesh, no breasts, no pubis. Nothing. I am artificial. Metal and wire and cord all over.

In the Pod I feel no pain.

I flex my fingers and the missile pods cycle.

I turn my head

and the Pod changes direction.

But where is my body? Why am I still linked to it? Am I cursed with an eternal body? Is my brain my body too? What am I? Who am I?

Explosions in space so dark the stars are diamond-eye-piercing bright, but they are dying or dead stars. We only see the light, much much later. My Pod, my body, moves through nothing. I can only hear the sounds of my Pod. The alien ship chases me, like a comet tail, like a very hungry bristling sea urchin with long black spikes. Comet. Falling star. Bad luck. I spin, dodge and spin again. I feel dizzy. My body is steel. I should not be feeling dizzy. I shouldn't be. I am healthy. I am healthy. Colors light up. Beeps and shrieks of the Pod echoing in and through me. My body is screaming at me. Evasive manoeuvres! Turn, turn, turn! Flee! I am the Pod. I am invincible.

Flee, flee, flee! All my instincts are shrieking. Flee!

A sharp pain lances down my spine. I have been shot!

But I have no spine.

I have no actual body.

My body is metal and wire.

I am linked. I am me. I am the Pod.

I am no warrior.

I am going down, down, down.

The moon looms before me. A new moon, unknown, nameless.

I think of home, of my wife, of my little girl, of her little flower bracelets.

꩜

I am going to land.
terra firma, solid ground.
land now, just land.

꩜

I hope to remain calm –
consistent, sure as the tides
and as violent as rip currents that pull me
apart,
tear me inside out,
outside in.

꩜

I have landed.
My moon.
My home.

—fin—

Being Invisible

"The Lessons of the Moon" (published in *Accessing The Future: A Disability-Themed Anthology of Speculative Fiction*, edited by Djibril al-Ayad and Kathryn Allan) is in part a story about me and my body. How I coped with loss and disappointment, and the realization that I am disabled. I wrote a protagonist who chooses, in their pain, to become an alien-destroying machine. Part of me yearned so much to be a cyborg or a machine, because my physical body seemed (seems) to be failing me.

I have an invisible disability. No, let's make that "invisible disabilities." I pass as normal/able-bodied, but I will let you in on a secret: I was diagnosed with hypertension when I was sixteen. Since then, I have been on anti-hypertension medication. Because of my hypertension, my two pregnancies were "high risk," coupled with placenta previa. Because of the trauma from my first pregnancy, I also became depressed.

When I was about 39-40, I had granulomatous mastitis which is basically non-cancerous growth in my breast. I was put on steroids by my surgeon. There began the slow, painful, and exhausting healing/recovery process which wreaked havoc on my body, both physically and emotionally. Because of the steroids, I was advised to go off my anti-depressants. That was not fun.

And because of the prolonged medication, I now have mild fatty liver which I am told is reversible with a strict (read "restricted") diet. Steroids and painkillers, thanks.

So, my disabilities are invisible. They are also chronic illnesses I have to deal with for the rest of my life. When I was younger, still shocked by the diagnosis of hypertension, I thought I was truly hampered by this illness. I was weak. *Why me? Why now? Why these limits? Why am I trapped within this failing chunk of flesh?* It didn't help that the incredibly sensitive and tactful specialist (not) told me, point blank, that I might just stroke out and die.

Well done, sir. You just frightened a teenager shitless with their future right before them. I changed specialists. My new doctor didn't have the manners of a brick. I stopped taking bad medical advice, took up tennis, and grew confident. I wrote in school publications. I was happy. I took my medications. I didn't stroke out. I simply learned to live with the new limits of my body.

Most people who meet me will never know how firm or sudden those limits can be, especially when I'm experiencing a bout of fatigue. When I was recovering from granulomatous mastitis, I struggled with bone-deep fatigue when trying to teach at the same time. I would be writing my lesson plans, teaching 14-year-olds in the morning, and the bone-deep fatigue would remind me about my limits. I would go home by the end of the school day, my body feeling hollowed-out. There were good and bad days. I cherished the good days and loathed the bad days because bad days meant *I am not productive, I can't write, I can't live normally.* I was just blah. My breast surgeon laughed when I told him about this and said that I was his first patient who experienced all the bad side-effects. I was not amused. I did get better. For now, I have annual mammograms done and a yearly appointment to see him.

The hypertension is still there, like a caged and tamed beast. Somnolent and subdued by the meds at most times, I have to watch it lest it bare its fangs and claws.

Part of myself coping with all this came out when I wrote "The Lessons of the Moon". My frustration and sadness wove into the story. I hated my body. I still tear up when I think about the writing process for the story. In fact, I wrote the poem on the day I had my biopsy done. My left breast burned as if it was on fire. The local anesthesia didn't work. My breast tissue was just too inflamed, according to the surgeon. She was very kind and understanding. After the biopsy, I went to my parents' to recuperate. In the silence of my dad's study room, I wrote. In the rest of the story that followed, the pain and disappointment throbbed as undercurrents. As an alien-killing machine, the protagonist is finally free . . . or are they? Have they made the right choice? Having a cyborg body is tempting, immensely so. Yet, is being part-machine or all-machine the best solution to my problems? Will all my illnesses go away?

It will come back, my breast surgeon reminded me. It will come back. It's just hiding now, like the hypertension. Cowed, but defiantly clinging on.

My disabilities are invisible. In my country, they are not even considered disabilities. Just chronic and auto-immune illnesses to be managed by healthcare providers. Healthcare's getting more expensive too. I can't help but wonder if I'm now a liability in the long run. Carpal tunnel syndrome. Rheumatoid arthritis. They just keep on piling up.

My wish is that people with invisible disabilities would speak up more. We pass as able-bodied. Our bodies remind us otherwise that we are not. Writing "The Lessons of the Moon" taught me that we need to have more SF/F stories about disability, especially invisible disabilities. The story contains my silent anxiety about having an invisible illness which doesn't really go away, but will only deteriorate over time. May genre fiction hear more of our voices.

I Found Love In An Urn Full Of Ashes

I found love in an urn full of ashes.

It was unexpected, as usual. Love is always unexpected. My trusted retainer, Fu Xi, came to me, head bowed respectfully. It was twilight, the time between day and night—I stirred from my bed. The vines above whispered in the unseen breezes that often coursed through my cave kingdom.

"My august lord," Fu Xi lowered his head even further, his ears canted forward. "The stars have matched, the felicitations are in order. You have a concubine waiting for your pleasure."

I sat up, tying my robes, tugging hard at the belt. My heart quickened. For a long time, I had been lonely and alone. Did the stars indeed match?

"Show me," I growled. Fu Xi bowed again and trotted off, his claws clicking on the stone floor. His orders sent the echoes twisting and turning against the cave walls. The army of bats, my other eyes, rustled and flapped their wings in agitation. My cave kingdom had begun to wake.

It was a brown urn, beautiful in its simplicity. No designs, no whorls, nothing. Just an urn, curved like two joined hands. Small enough for me to cup in my own large paws.

"The matchmaker said this is the best match," Fu Xi's fox eyes gleamed. "I trust her judgment and have sent her away with the adequate payment. My Lord?" He inclined his head gently.

"We will have the ceremony the next nightfall," I licked my

lips. Would she be beautiful? Would she shy away from my bestial sight?

༺☾༻

The entire cave kingdom gathered for the wedding ceremony. The bats escorted the foxes, the deer, the spiders, the snakes and even the lowest toads to the Great Hall, chittering away as they flew above the heads of the guests, guiding and scolding them at the same time. The snake women hid their smiles behind their long sleeves, their eyes shining with speculation. The spider women clustered together, weaving their silk idly. I had already received their tribute of the best-spun spider silk robes, a wedding gift for my bride. The foxes readied their instruments of cymbals and pipes, ready to greet my bride when she appeared.

Fu Xi even procured a Taoist priest spirit for the wedding. He would prevent my bride from fleeing. Ideally, the matchmaker should be here, but she had already fled the kingdom. Humans are such fragile creatures, easily frightened and unaccustomed to our ways. But my new bride would be human too, albeit now in spirit form.

At the right moment, when the stars aligned and the moon crossed the aegis, the Taoist priest broke the seal of the urn and whispered the words that would free the spirit within, the spirit of my bride.

Wisps of white smoke swirled out of the broken urn, forming the shape of a slender human figure. At first, the figure seemed to be kneeling down, before unfolding like a cloth puppet. Features sharpened. I heard the watching animals gasp.

I stared. The eyes of the white figure opened. They were luminous. Beside me, Fu Xi shrank a little.

The young scholar shook his head and looked around, bemusedly. "Where the hell am I?"

"You are now married," intoned the Taoist priest who then dissipated because his job was done. The words lingered in the suddenly cold air of the Great Hall. Some of the snake women looked as if they were about to faint. The band of fox musicians started playing a wedding song. With a glare from Fu Xi, they stopped, the song tapering into a few discordant notes. Someone blew an out-of-tune pipe and descended immediately into an embarrassed silence.

"I—," I looked at my right wrist and baulked. Red thread glowed between it and the young scholar's hand. He looked at me in amazement.

The young man, his eyes like phoenix eyes, his lips full and mobile, began to laugh merrily. "Looks like I am now married to you, lord." He wasn't afraid of me.

He wasn't afraid of me.

The wedding banquet was an uncomfortable occasion with the guests visibly shaken by the revelation that my bride was actually my bride-groom. I scowled into my cup of wine, knowing that after this, the rumors would go out into the wild, carried by eager tongues and to even more eager ears. I might have well stood at the peak of the tallest mountain and roared the news out to the wind.

My bride-groom picked at the plates of delicacies laid out before him. By now he had solidified enough to hold his chopsticks. My cooks had worked hard for the feast: tiny goldfish-shaped buns filled with lotus seed paste, bowls of clear savory soup with river clams and prawns, osmanthus jelly cut into jewel-liked shapes in which the precious flower petals hung suspended as if in amber.

"But I am a spirit," he said very clearly, very loudly. "How can I eat?"

"Just inhale its essence," I said sternly and immediately regretted my harsh tone. The scholar glanced at me and shrugged. He sniffed at the jelly, his expression turning into one of joy. I found myself staring at him, at his beauty. He was a very hand-some man.

۞

Fu Xi abased himself before me. My fox lieutenant knelt, his ears flat against his skull.

I was distracted. How was I supposed to go through with the wedding night?

"I apologize," Fu Xi stammered. "The matchmaker promised me that it was a perfect match."

"Forget it, Fu Xi," I snapped. "It has been a mistake."

I left Fu Xi still kneeling on the cold stone floor. Not surprisingly I found my bride-groom browsing in my large library, his slender fingers caressing the rolled-up scrolls tenderly. He was itching to read all of them. He started and turned around, his face at once embarrassed and surprised. He looked like a startled deer, caught in a snare of light and sound.

"It's all yours," I said, gesturing at the entire span of the library with my right paw.

"My lord," the young scholar blinked, laughing softly. "That would be extravagant of you."

"I am lord of this realm," I declared. "Everything that is mine is yours."

The young scholar hid a smile behind his very elegant hand. His eyes sparkled. His scrutiny made me uncomfortable. "You have the original copy of *The Romance of the Red Chamber*, and a first-edition copy of *Journey To The West*. And the Heart, Diamond and Lotus Sutras!" he gestured excitedly. His joy lifted me, so much joy.

"I was match-made to you," he continued, caressing my large dark-wood table and the brushes, "and you hardly knew my name."

I drew myself to my full height. "I am Lord Tian Mu Sin, tiger lord of the cave kingdom of Hei Shan, dread master of the animal demons."

"A tiger lord," the young scholar said. "Fascinating."

My voice caught painfully in my throat. I was falling in love with the young scholar. "What is your name?"

"Me? I am Kai Feng or *was*," the young scholar replied, a wry smile on his lips. "I died at the age of twenty, two days before the Imperial Examinations."

A hard lump formed in my stomach. Perhaps indeed it had been a mistake. A big mistake. I opened my mouth to speak, but Kai Feng's eyes stopped me. They were wide with fear. He knew what was coming.

"I won't hurt you," I said. "I promise."

I left Kai Feng asleep on the fur-covered bed, his body curled into a ball. I draped a fur blanket over his bare shoulders. Eyes closed, he looked as if he wanted to shut the world out. He smelled of the earth, of the sweetest of osmanthus flowers.

It was twilight. It was time for me to patrol the borders of my kingdom. Fu Xi kept a watchful eye on the Great Hall. I shrugged off my robes and flowed into my natural shape.

It was time to hunt.

Reports from Fu Xi and his fox soldiers painted a sobering picture of human incursions. Demonhunters were breaking past the wards; all the paper talismans had been ripped, slashed apart. I had recently taken to etching the spell words into the cave walls with a combination of my blood and the earth of the cave kingdom. These demonhunters were bold enough to breach them. In my natural form I prowled, sniffing out any traces of human sign, the golden silky lines that criss-crossed the cave network like . . .

Fox.

Fox.

Spider.

Snake.

Fox.

Human.

Human.

There was a human . . . a male who had pushed past the wards. Not my bride-groom. Different smell, different taste. Heavier, muskier, the hint of blood and fire, righteousness and pride. Demonhunter. I growled. I hated them. My growl seeped into the ground and shook the air. The vines rustled. The bats roosting squealed and flapped their wings in fear.

I lifted my head and roared my challenge. The wards flamed up, the characters burning with their own fire, curling and swirling. The bats screeched and left their roost in a burst of wings. They swarmed in the middle of the cave, in ever-tightening circles. When the wards shone with the light of dying stars, turning the insides of the cave into a reminder of the Eighteen Levels of Hell, the bats streamed out into the night, screaming their terror and warning the rest of Hei Shan of my wrath.

Resuming my form on two legs, I exhaled slowly, feeling the slow tugging drain in my blood and bones. Will working took energy from me. The wards needed reinforcing. I stretched my arms to the unseen sky and roared once more. Perspiration ran down my back, pooling at my clawed feet. The earth drank thirstily. The caves roared back at me. I soaked in the sound, my blood singing.

When I turned around, I saw the young scholar, wrapped in his furs, standing between the thorn bushes, hand on his mouth. I opened my own mouth to say something, to reason, to make excuses, to apologize. Without a word, he simply turned around and walked back into the darkness.

Kai Feng avoided me for a few days, keeping to himself. He stayed mostly in my study, reading the scrolls and writing on rice paper. I sent him choice delicacies from the kitchen: famous Xi An red dates stuffed with walnuts, honeyed figs dripping with syrup, and steamed barbecued pork buns. My table was strewn with rolls and rolls of calligraphy, elegant and graceful characters that flew across the paper like migrating geese.

He finally broke his silence one twilight.

I found him wandering down the corridor to our shared chamber; he had recently taken to sleeping in a separate bed chamber. He bowed respectfully, keeping a distance from me.

"You were terrifying," he said without preamble. "You were terrifying and I hated you for that."

I glanced at him mildly. Deep in accounts and matters of the kingdom, I didn't pay full attention to him.

"I was frightened," Kai Feng continued relentlessly. "I wanted to run away. Flee for my life. What manner of beast are you?"

Beast. The word hit me harder than I'd expected. I placed the brush down, sipped my tea and looked directly at him. He wore the spider silk gown made by the spider women. It hugged his hips, flowed from his body in a shimmering cascade of golden threads and red brocade. I rose from my chair. *Beast.*

"I am a tiger *demon*," I said slowly. "Everyone in this kingdom is a demon. A jin. We are beasts, because we cannot attain enlightenment just by reciting mere sutras. We are far from the fairies and fabled peaches in the Jade Emperor's Palace. But that does not make us less of any being in the Tao."

Kai Feng regarded me carefully. "Then what am I in the world of demons?" he asked, a small catch in his voice. "Where do I stand in this kingdom of jin and shape-changers?"

"You are my consort," I said quietly. "You stand at my right hand and sit at my table. The kingdom is also yours."

He lowered his eyes. "I see."

"Are you not happy?" I walked up to him, afraid to startle him. "Are you not pleased?" *He wanted to run away. He wanted to flee. I am a beast. Beast.*

What am I, but a Beast?

"I am comfortable and the foxes are fastidious in their care," Kai Feng shook his head at my approach, his raised hand drawing an invisible boundary between him and me. "I am just . . . getting used to all this attention. And to this place. Mainly to this place." He smiled weakly, shaking his head again.

"How can I make you more comfortable?" I said.

Kai Feng circled the chamber, his eyes admiring the scrolls stacked neatly on the shelves, his hands caressing the rosewood. Such a tactile person. His gaze then lingered on the bed, before he sighed and closed his eyes.

When he opened them again, they were bright and unwavering. "How can you make me more comfortable? I am not sure, my august lord. I died, and then I am here. I am not the same person I used to be. I grapple, my lord, with this new reality. And . . . I am at a loss."

I ached to hold him in my arms. "What can I do?"

"Treat me as an equal. Remind me of who I am. Let me be."

I heard the bats chittering softly, as if they added their voices in agreement. Somewhere someone howled, a sad and lonely sound in the cave kingdom. I also knew that Fu Xi was listening in, intently. The foxes were everywhere. The cave network was their familiar ground. Whatever I said would be communicated through the kingdom, because my word was law. I had to choose my words very carefully.

"You are my equal. From this day forth, the animals will listen to you. Your word is my word."

Kai Feng's eyes pinned me down where I stood. I felt naked before him. "Promise me that this is true. I am nobody's chattel. Promise me!"

"I promise."

So my word was law.

⁂

When Kai Feng flew into my study, I knew something was wrong.

The nape of my neck bristled. My fur stood. For a whole week, things went horribly wrong. The wards were ruined again. The springs ran dry, the first time in many thousand years. The eggs of the spider women had not hatched, breaking a generations-old cycle. Two days ago, while on patrol, Fu Xi found a clutch of dead baby snakes: frozen and drained of blood. The snake women buried them with much wailing and beating of chests.

Kai Feng's eyes were wild, his skin wan. Even his immaculate long hair, kept tightly bound with a silver clasp, hung loose. I noticed that his dark blue scholar robes were open at the front. It was out of character for the neat and fastidious Kai Feng to not pay attention to his physical appearance. Every twilight, he would stand before the mirror so that he could comb his hair, making sure it was neat and tidy. Smooth, it resembled black silk. His habit grew into a pleasant pattern. I would watch him clasp his hair with a certain pleasure. He would smile shyly at me.

"My august lord," he blurted out, "I think I might be pregnant."

I burst out laughing. It was absurd. It was too absurd. "You are male and should not be pregnant. Perhaps you have eaten something that disagreed with you."

Kai Feng rolled his eyes at me. "You are not listening, my lord. I think I might be pregnant. Yes, I know I am male and I do not possess the parts to bear a child. But I felt kicks in my stomach. I felt hands and feet. I have not been feeling well for a month now."

I did notice Kai Feng not touching his favorite delicacies for the past few days. He did look usually pale. Even now while he stood, his hand held onto the edge of the table for balance.

"I opened my robes today to see this . . ." Kai Feng pulled apart the front of his robes. His stomach glowed, as if a small sun resided within his body. I could see the outline of a head and feet stirring in the amber light.

"I . . ." I said and couldn't find the words to continue.

"The heavens are playing tricks on me," Kai Feng sighed, closing his robes, shivering. "This is impossible."

I drew him into my arms. The prospect of myself as a father unnerved me.

The child grew rapidly. Kai Feng was alternately angry, happy, and ravenously hungry. A harried Fu Xin ran in and out, up and down, the kingdom, to find the food my bride-groom wanted. He craved longan fruit. He demanded more red dates stuffed with walnuts, this time dipped in fresh honey. At one time, he wanted to eat deep fried spiders sprinkled with five-spices. That became a point of contention amongst the spider folk who drew the line between eating kin and not-kin. He moved on to steamed frog legs with finely-sliced ginger and wolfberries, stripping the white meat from the tiny bones with relish. In a fit of nostalgia, he requested for bin tang hu lu, sugared haw fruits skewered in sticks. He ate and ate and ate. His stomach grew and grew.

The pregnancy seemed to give Kai Feng energy too. He drew, did calligraphy, and read scroll after scroll. His intellectual appetite was as boundless as his physical cravings.

On the night of Mid-Autumn, when the moon was large and full in the sky, its white light cast on the cave kingdom's many-layered tiers, Kai Feng complained about severe pangs in his stomach. It bulged taut, the skin straining. When I touched it, it burned my fingers. Without hesitation, I carried him to our bedchamber.

He groaned and cursed, the pain turning my gentle Kai Feng into a swearing sweating beast, while the child struggled to be free of its confines. I brought in a snake midwife who wrung her hands and watched on helplessly. "This is beyond my expertise, my lord," she wept while Kai Feng cried out. The child seemed to have its own ideas. Light began to issue forth from Kai Feng's navel. As Kai Feng yelled, the navel seemed to widen and the tip of the baby's head emerged. Inch by inch, the head appeared, the baby's face scrunched up. The midwife leaned forward and coaxed the child out. The rest of the body slipped out. There was no umbilical cord, no placenta. It was after all the child of a spirit man and a tiger lord.

And my son—my *son*—roared his first roar. His cry echoed in the chamber. The midwife wrapped him up in swathing cloths. She quickly handed him over Kai Feng who cried happy tears. He wept: "It's a son, our son, our son."

"Your son, my lord," the midwife announced, beaming away, her forked tongue flickering.

My son. Our son.

I gently eased the baby over into my arms. Feather-light, he had tiger ears with tuffs of wispy fur and the faintest suggestion of stripes along his arms and legs. His skin was translucent, fragile to the touch. Blue veins coursed through his body. Kai Feng's eyes stared back at me.

While Kai Feng rested, I carried our son to the window looking out into the forest lands beneath. The moon danced in the sky. Demon children carried lit lanterns as they sang songs. The parade faded into the darkness.

"I will name you Tian Min," I whispered to the baby his name, his promise. "Sky Bright, Sky Bright."

Barely three months passed before Kai Feng became pregnant again. This time, in the deep cold, the night before Winter Solstice, our daughter was born. I called her Tian Xin. Sky Star. She had stripes like her older brother and more pronounced canine teeth.

The entire kingdom rippled with the news and gossip. I didn't care. I had my children. I was proud of Kai Feng. It was a delightful surprise and pure joy to hold our two children in my arms. The elders of the spider, snake and fox tribes talked about reincarnation and Heaven's Will, about souls and being assigned different forms. But this was my kingdom, a kingdom of jin, demons and shape-changers, far from the lofty ideals of the Jade Palace. My children had a place in the path of the Tao. They bore celestial names. I wished with all my heart they would reach the sky and beyond.

We celebrated their full moon months with much fanfare. Every household in the cave kingdom was given two eggs coated with red edible dye and sweetmeats. The fox musicians sang songs written in honor of Tian Min and Tian Xin.

At night, we slept with the two babies curled up in our arms. I, tiger lord of the cave kingdom of Hei Shan, a father of two children. It was a time of peace and contentment, something which I had not known for a while now.

New demonhunter incursions broke our two months of bliss.

✦

Fu Xi found the wards guarding the cave mouth leading to the kingdom desecrated by black ink and sword slashes. The hunter was particularly destructive so much so that the wards actually dissipated. What dark heart actually beat in that chest? Was the demonhunter even real?

"Protect our children," Kai Feng dug his fingers into my arm. He cast worried glances at the two sleeping babies. "I have an awful feeling he's after our children."

"Nonsense," I tried to soothe him, but my heart clenched. "He is probably after the demons in our kingdom. Perhaps even after me."

Kai Feng rested his head against my chest. "Please do not say that. I want to protect you too."

He pushed away suddenly—an idea had struck him—and

looked hard into my eyes. "Teach me how to use a jian or a bow and arrows. Let me protect you and the children."

He plunged into the jian drills diligently. A quick and observant learner, Kai Feng picked the skills rapidly and was soon performing his drills flawlessly while I watched. How would he cope with a real attacker? Demonhunters were wily and ruthless. They would kill him. They would kill us.

They would kill our children.

❧

The ferocity of the blade plunged towards me. It was a hateful thing, that blade. Dipped in blood, my blood, Kai Feng's blood, it thirsted more. The man behind the blade had a contorted face filled with righteous rage. After all, we were just demons to him. Only his kind had the right to exist and live. He roared challenges at me. He screamed condemnations at me. He cursed my ancestors and the entire lineage of tigers before me.

"I am Lord Guan, Protector of Lives and Killer of Demons," he growled and it was such a bitter growl. I wondered about the origins of his bitterness. Had he not loved? Had he not offered kindness, compassion and generosity? "You are an unholy pestilence, a plague on the land."

I stood my ground, my claws in a defensive pose, my saber pointed at him. What did he see? A tiger lord, fangs bared, eyes glowing. A demon?

"I was commissioned to kill you, you sender of disease and illness. Your head will be on a platter. I will be a champion."

He was talking too much.

"Bag of hot air," I said, chuckling as if one of my courtiers had made a joke. "Cease talking."

The demonhunter's eyes widened, the jibe struck home. He lunged forward with his blade . . .

And I woke, gasping hard for air. Kai Feng had his arm draped across my chest, but even then he stirred, feeling the echoes of my dream. I had not dreamed such dreams for a long time now. Chilled to the bone, I realized I dreamed my own death.

I gently removed Kai Feng's arm, stroking it before I placed it back on his bare body. Sighing deeply, I swung my feet out of the bed. I was already weary. Tian Xin gurgled and waved her chubby fists. I walked to the cradle and picked her up. She waved her arms vigorously, her smile a bright light in our bedchambers. I held her close.

"Had a bad dream?" Soft as Kai Feng's voice was, it made me jump.

"Tiger lords do not dream," I lied, putting Tian Xin back into her cradle. She squealed and looked very disappointed. It was hard to stay unhappy with her.

Kai Feng sat up, his long hair half-hiding his face. He wrapped the furs around his shoulders. "You were muttering in your sleep."

"So I mutter in my sleep," I tried to sound as if I was teasing him. The pit of my stomach was ice-cold. "That doesn't mean I dream."

"You also snore," Kai Feng smiled playfully. "But you will keep denying it."

"Tiger lords do not snore nor do they dream," I countered, pulling on my robes. I needed to move. I needed to run in my natural form. "We are magical beings. Dreams are for the mortal souls."

Kai Feng's look told me that he knew I was lying. I had to be honest with him. He wanted me to treat him as an equal. He sat beside me in Court. I had to speak the truth.

"I dreamed of my death," I said. There I said it. It was out in the open, the words flying home. Kai Feng's face became still, his hands slowly curling into fists. Everything grew silent, except for the gurgling and squealing of our children.

"That was not hard to say, wasn't it?" Kai Feng said. He left the bed too and joined me where I stood immobile, frightened by my own truth. It loomed large and invisible, demanding to be confronted.

I took his hands into mine, lifting them to my lips. "I am afraid, my love. Afraid that I might die and lose you."

"I will defend you," Kai Feng said fiercely. In his nakedness, he had never looked so brave, so courageous. Who was I to deserve him? "I will fight, because I too am a warrior, a man."

Wordlessly, I gathered him into my arms. He was so warm, so soft. We made love, our hands on our bodies, our mouths on skin and limb. We lay entwined on the floor of our bedchamber, inflamed like suns in union.

It was the only thing we could do.

Kai Feng made sure that the babies stayed close to him. He was adamant he had a jian with him, with a unit of fox soldiers attached to him for protection. He was also adamant that I had my bodyguards with me at all times.

Then Tian Xin disappeared.

Tian Xin matured faster than her older brother. She was already toddling on her two feet before he rolled over on his stomach. Soon she was walking about, her hand holding onto any surface, any stone, any edge, resisting any help from Kai Feng or me or any of the maidservants who marveled at her independence and yet rued it at the same time.

One of the maids, a willowy fox girl, rushed up to me, her tears streaking down her face in dark rivulets. "My lord, my lord, she is gone. Gone."

"Who is gone, girl?" I snapped.

"Your thousand gold, your beloved daughter, our most beloved princess . . ."

I ignored her and ran towards the garden where Kai Feng was. I found him in the middle of a swirling mass of panicking soldiers and maidservants. He looked furious, his hand holding a jian, his hair whipping about.

"He took her," Kai Feng hissed. "HE TOOK HER."

"Who? Who took her?"

The fox soldiers began to wail and yank at their fur, while the maidservants screamed their horror.

"I will kill him! I will truly kill him!" Kai Feng raged, glaring at me. "I will find him, I will tear him from limb to limb."

Fu Xi groveled towards me, his ears flattened against his skull. "He broke through the wards, my lord. Our security is now compromised."

"The demonhunter," I said and my anger turned the air to

snow. The soldiers stopped their wailing and huddled together, staring helplessly at the drifting white flakes. The maidservants sobbed as snow covered everything in white and cold. *"The demonhunter dies now."*

In my rage, I towered over my love. My war form was huge, muscular. I glimpsed it mirrored on the frost-covered cave walls. Beast. Beast. Beast.

Kai Feng held me back. "But you will get yourself killed." The dream echoed between us, the dream of myself dying under the blade of the demonhunter . . . who had taken my baby daughter.

"He took something of mine. He took our daughter. I will kill him. I WILL KILL HIM."

So, without looking back at him, I leaped forward and bounded into the twilight.

"Mu Sin . . . Tian Mu Sin!" Kai Feng called frantically. " Tian Mu Sin!" His voice dwindled into the distance. The blood roared in my ears. I could not hear him.

I followed the trail of the demonhunter, a pulsating path of blood and burning that crossed streams and climbed up the walls of the cave kingdom. If hate had a scent, it would be burning, a distillation of destruction into a scent. It crawled up my nose and seared my senses. My blood boiled. This was the criminal who kidnapped my daughter.

And Tian Xin was a soft golden glowing orb that kept apart from the blood and burning. It bounced like a ball of marsh gas, but it did not merge with that hate-scent of the demonhunter. I was relieved to know that she was still alive. What could a demonhunter do to a half-spirit, half-tiger child?

I cut his escape route by the time twilight descended upon the caves.

He was … an old man with unkempt black hair and bristling beard. Armor of the current human dynasty covered his large body. His eyes were wild, inflamed with the passion of self-righteousness. A large halberd, tipped with a fearsome blade, accompanied his relentless stride. A cloth bag bulged on his left side. It swung heavily. I could see the shape of a baby's body inside. As I prowled closer, I saw the imprint of tiny hands and legs. My rage burst forth in my heart. My daughter, ill-treated like that, carried like ordinary food or clothing. The time for hiding was over. I padded out of the bushes, growling threats and curses at the demonhunter.

"DEMON!" The old man shouted and dropped the cloth bag. My heart dropped. Was Tian Xin hurt? Did she injure herself? How dare he …

He drew the halberd in a semi-circle, carving the air with it. I drew myself to my full height, my body resuming its two-legged form. My muscles strained. I longed to kill him. Without hesitation, he lunged at me. The ferocity of the blade plunged towards me. It was a hateful thing, that blade. Dipped in blood, it thirsted more. The man behind the blade had a contorted face filled with righteous rage. After all, we were just demons to him. Only his kind had the right to exist and live. He roared challenges at me.

He screamed condemnations at me. He cursed my ancestors and the entire lineage of tigers before me.

"I am Lord Guan, Protector of Lives and Killer of Demons," he growled and it was such a bitter growl. I wondered about the origins of his bitterness. Had he not loved? Had he not offered kindness, compassion and generosity? "You are an unholy pestilence, a plague on the land."

I stood my ground, my claws in a defensive pose, my saber pointed at him. What did he see? A tiger lord, fangs bared, eyes glowing? A demon? I realized I was acting my dream out now and a chill went up my back. Could I stop fate? Was I destined to die by the blade of a demonhunter?

"I was commissioned to kill you, you sender of disease and illness. Your head will be on a platter. I will be a champion, celebrated and adored by many."

He was talking too much.

"Bag of hot air," I said, chuckling as if one of my courtiers had joked. "Cease talking."

The demonhunter's eyes widened, the jibe struck home. He swore and flew towards me with the halberd. I deflected it with my saber. The blades burned bright as the edges hissed and cut at each other. He kicked at me, trying to throw me off balance. I ducked, reached out and hooked his thigh with my killing claw. Blood spurted, a flowering of deep red like the groves of pomegranates in bloom that flourished close to the forest ringing Hei Shan. I quickly drew back while he sagged and tried to stem the blood from the wound with his hands.

"Hideous tiger," he spat.

Chuckling, he said the *word*.

Demonhunters were also sorcerers, trained in arts darker than the Taoist priests. They often entailed the use of blood and body parts, as blood and meat were more binding, deeply insidious than mere words. The word he used was a blood word that turned my veins cold, my bones into frozen icicles and rendered my entire body immobile. I crashed onto the earth, unable to react, unable to even scream. I could only stare at the demonhunter coming towards me, his victorious smirk a slap to my face. He bled still, but he walked with the stride of a cocky man so assured of his fortune.

He lowered the blade tip of the halberd and I smelled blood. A lot of it. The blade had drunk deep. It inched now along my throat. I could only stare at him, wishing all the hate I had at him. In the back of my mind, I thought of Kai Feng, of his gentle smile and fierce heart, of Tian Min.

That my kingdom would just end with a stroke of a demon-hunter's blade.

Would he kill Kai Feng then and destroy the rest of my beloved people? Would their souls even forgive me for my failure to protect them?

I waited for the blade to slice into my neck, praying for a quick death. Instead, I heard gagging. I thought I was gagging, but I was still breathing, still whole. It was the demonhunter squeezing his throat with his two hands as if he was strangling himself. In truth, he was being strangled. His halberd had fallen beside him.

Craning my neck, the process painful as the spell still bound me, I saw Tian Xin, out of the cloth bag, her chubby fists waving in the air. She looked like she was trying to catch the iridescent soap bubbles blown by her maidservants. She shook her fist and the demonhunter choked even harder. With a determined look on her little face, she pounded her fist on the ground. The demonhunter fell onto his knees, the whites of his eyes showing. He gagged for one last time, before collapsing on his side.

Slowly, I pushed myself off the ground. The spell had worn off. My body hurt. It truly hurt. Toddling on my weak legs, I stumbled over to the demonhunter. He still breathed. I saw a beautiful porcelain pendant with blue and white peonies, lying askew on his chest. It looked too fragile, too delicate.

Tian Xin laughed happily when I finally held her in my arms, kicking out in excitement. My daughter saved me. What other talents did she hide in her body?

I heard running feet and the hint of *Kai Feng*—before my love crashed out of the shrubs, wearing armor and dressed like a warrior. A unit of fox soldiers, similarly dressed, followed him. Fu Xi stalked beside Kai Feng, bearing his own blade. They all skidded to a halt when they saw the unconscious demonhunter.

"Tian Xin!" Kai Feng cried, rushing forward. He grabbed our daughter and held her close against his chest. Laughing, he pulled me to him. I encircled Kai Feng with my arms, relieved to see him. I inhaled his scent and it filled my heart with joy.

"Is he dead?" Kai Feng whispered as the fox soldiers checked the demonhunter all over and removed his weapons. He had daggers and gunpowder balls tucked into many pockets inside his armor. They took them away, including the halberd. Fu Xi had him stripped of his armor. I instructed to leave the pendant be. Fu Xi looked at me as if I had grown an extra head.

"I want him dumped at the border, where the xiong nu lives. Let them deal with him," I said. "I heard they do not take kindly to strangers in their land." Saluting smartly, the fox soldiers dragged the demonhunter away. They had bound his hands and legs with thorn-rope. The thorns bit into flesh and could never be removed.

"How did you—?" Kai Feng nuzzled Tian Xin.

"Tian Xin saved me," I replied. "Our daughter has magical powers."

Kai Feng's laughter was infectious. The caves echoed with the sound. "Really?"

"She's after all the child of a spirit and a tiger lord," I grinned. "Anything could happen."

The entire kingdom celebrated our return with fanfare. The fox musicians played rousing tunes with their cymbals and pipes, beating their drums to greet us when we walked towards the Great Hall, Tian Xin in my arms, Kai Feng at my side. The spider women wove glittering banners that spanned the cave walls like a sky full of stars. Even the fireflies emerged for this grand occasion. Everybody danced to the music.

Tian Xin quickly grew bored of the attention and fell asleep on Kai Feng's lap. Tian Min, upon seeing his sister's return and the maidservants lavishing all their care on her, started to howl indignantly. We chuckled and I swung him into the air. Suspended by my arms, he began to giggle and kick his legs vigorously. We pretended we were the powerful giant eagles that flew at the top of Hei Shan, carried by the winds and lifted by their large wings. Halfway through our play, ghostly white wings appeared on

Tian Min's back. Perhaps that was his gift. One day, he would fly, perhaps even higher than the eagles.

We played until Tian Min yawned and rubbed his eyes irritably, a sign he was tired and wanted to sleep.

Fed on rich goat's milk and content, our two children fell asleep in their cradles. I held Kai Feng's hand while we stared out into the cave kingdom laid out beneath us. The celebration was still winding across all the different levels of the cave network.

Kai Feng exhaled softly as he glanced across our chamber. His gaze rested upon the brown urn on one of the shelves, right beside the scrolls of mythical and historical heroes and generals. One of his favorite stories was the Yang clan of women generals who rode into war.

"Do you think it's a mistake?" he said, placing his hand on my arm, a tender pressure that spoke so much more.

"Do you?" I asked. Someone let loose firecrackers. The maidservants tut-tutted and darted frantic looks at Tian Min and Tian Xin. They slept on, barely stirring at the sharp crackling sounds. Tian Min could be difficult when he did not get enough sleep.

Kai Feng brushed his topknot self-consciously before shaking his head. "I do not. I think I love you." His lips brushed against my throat. "I love you."

My heart sang.

I finally found love.

—fin—

Diary of War

1.

I am awake. The war hasn't arrived yet.

It is sunny, complete with blue skies and white wispy clouds.

Outside Mama is hanging the laundry. She loves the
'sun-smell' on clean clothes.

I am reluctant to get out of bed.

 In two days' time, I will turn

sixteen.

Most of my peers have gone off to the academies.

2.

Mama is not at home today.

She's gone off to the town council meeting to vote. Our town
tithes two regiments of soldiers. Half of the town has

lost sons, brothers, husbands.

Daughters, sisters, wives too.

We argued last night.

 I should be at the frontline. Mama protested. She was angry.

Her eyes blazed like fire.

Her eyes always blaze

like fire.

I get out of the room. On the table, still faintly steaming, is

a bowl of hand-pulled noodles and two hard-boiled eggs.

The broth is savory.

My birthday treat.

3.

There was the sound of explosions in the distance, near the town of Sweetherb.

The siren pierced through the air.

It was in the middle of the night.

Some people ran out into the streets.

It is quiet when I wake in the morning. Mama sleeps deeply.

She returned from her meeting angry, her lips

in a thin straight line.

I find myself harvesting the herbs from the wasteland.

Some herbs are in Mama's book. Some herbs are new and I have to go check. I dry some of them next to the big window.

They smell good.

4.

The explosions were loud enough to shake us out of bed.

The air smelled like gunpowder

from the New Year fireworks display.

It got into my nose, on to my tongue. It is a taste hard to get rid of.

For the whole night, I thought of New Year food and that there would be no New Year this year.

We have not celebrated New Year ever since Baba left for the frontline.

I can't sleep.

I stare out of the window and it is

then I see it.

It has jade-green front claws that look like scythes and a shell-like body that gleams a paler green. While it moves, I see the smudges of organs moving inside the shell.

The eyes are large, set in front. I am reminded of

a praying mantis in Mama's books.

Except this is bigger, faster, more lean. It moves up the street, its front claws twitching as if they are tasting the air.

Something booms further down and the green thing leaps towards it, its shell-body pulsing.

I clap my mouth shut. It is one of

the invaders.

They are here

in my town.

5.

Mama shakes me awake later. I have fallen asleep under the bed.

This time, Mama is wearing something different. She has army fatigues on, like the ones worn by the tithed regiments.

Yet the badges are not the same.

There is a long knife hanging from her belt.

Here, take this, she hands me a gun. I recognize its make.

It's the same as Baba's. She told me that it was a pistol, the night he left for the frontline.

You will need to protect yourself, Mama says and her eyes blaze.

 I will teach you how to use this.

6.

When the invaders arrive, there is no resistance.

None.

The village yields like

fragile paper.

I cut my hair, shave my face and follow Mama.

We protect our own, Mama whispers to me, as if she is telling me

a story from her past of dragons, fox spirits and spiders on two legs.

My arm still aches from the shooting.

We join Mama's friends in the dark. We lay bombs and damage the invaders' engines. When they explode, we laugh and run away.

In our hiding place, we tell our stories and share hot soup in tins. Mama sits in her corner, the knife across her lap.

She stares into the dark, her eyes like banked fire.

I cannot sleep.

7.

The sound of the invaders is bone-chilling.

You hear their chittering first, before you see them. The one I have seen is a scout.

The warriors are frightening, larger and their scythe-claws sharper.

They hunt at night.

8.

We churn out posters, printed words on paper.

Paper, such an old-fashioned thing.

Like Mama's books. The posters speak of resistance, of fighting against the invaders. Fight them. Deny them. Cut off their claws.

FIGHT.

They are invaders.

They take our homes.

They are barbarians.

They are ruthless.

Hate them. Chase them out.

Fight.

9.

When your land is invaded, what can you do?

What should you do?

Mama brings me to raids. I am glad for the darkness. Nobody questions me how I look.

Young boy. Young girl. I am both.

Under the camo paint, I am just part of the resistance. I streak green and black on my cheeks with relish.

We throw home-made bombs, made with distilled alcoholic spirit and twists of paper, tossed out in empty bottles salvaged from an old factory.

When the invader ships explode,

we shout with glee.

10.

The warrior looks at me with those large eyes, its scythe-claws slashing the air. It has the color of early spring leaves and its innards throb like

one giant heart.

For a while, we stare.

I hold onto my gun. My hands tremble.

You are not male, the warrior pulses.

You can talk to me, I whisper. My voice flees.

Of course, I can, the warrior says with a hint of pride. Its voice is the rustling of dried grass in my head. It is a strange uncomfortable sensation. I am taakaki.

Taaka-what? I blink and this time, the warrior raises its claws. They look curved, dangerous, with crimson—our blood—coating its shell.

Up close, the warrior is more crab than insect.

A high-pitched screech distracts the warrior. Suddenly it hisses at me, its eyes unfriendly. The claws slice towards me.

Something hits it. A small explosion of shell, foul-smelling . . . blood? I drop onto my buttocks. Mama comes running up, her face twisted in

a snarl, her gun pointed straight at the warrior.

The warrior chitters and backs away, finally scurrying off to whatever had summoned it.

Did it hurt you? Mama demands. I have the green blood on my uniform. Its stench makes me want to vomit.

I shake my head.

All I feel is dried grass in it, rustling, hissing.

11.

Taakaki.

The word/sensation/feeling lingers in my head. I dream of it. I dream of the warrior with its scythe-like claws.

Taakaki.

We bomb more invader ships. Our camp is victorious and we celebrate with rice cakes and wine. Somewhere, in a parallel peaceful planet,

we celebrate the return of spring.

It has gone bitterly cold. The snow coats everything in its sight.

I want to see plants, sprouting greens and herbs.

Taakaki.

The invader has planted

a seed in me.

12.

Silence.

13.

I wake in a cell.

14.

The seed is growing.

15.

We interrupt this diary for an important message:

The seed is growing.

Identity is real.

Fighting the invader is real.

16.

I wake in a cell.

It is cold. I am swimming in a clear gel.

A pulsating cord extends from my belly and ends in a gelatinous mess at my feet. It reminds me of the masses of frog eggs in the pond next to the wasteland.

I am also naked, all of me laid bare.

But I am too in pain to care, to protest.

17.

Who are you?

What are you?

I am who I am.

You are neither male nor female.

I am who I am.

18.

When they release me, I fall out of the cell in a rush of gel, blood and fluids, curled up, shivering. I have changed.

They change me.

My hands are now scythe claws, pink in color, shading into a dark green. But the rest of my body is still fleshy human. My nipples tingle in the sudden chill.

But my face . . . my face is half invader, my eyes grown larger, brighter, like an insect's. My hair is now chitin, pink-green, green-pink.

You are taakaki, the voice in my head says, rustling like dried grass. In between, neither. Now may you speak for us.

I am not your voice, I scream back.

I am not your plaything.

But you are, because we made you the way you are.

I cry, but my crying is the chittering of an insect.

Unmake me. I am not your puppet. You are evil, evil, evil. Change me back!

The dried-grass voice rustles and laughs.

19.

There are many voices. They echo and echo, a rush of high and low tones. In the hive, they resonate. It seems that the hive has been infiltrated.

I see her first.

Mama.

I try to speak up, my voice choking in my throat—

Mama!

She raises her pistol at me. The long knife in her other hand gleams with bright green. Blood of the invader. My blood.

Yao jin!

Her words are weapons. Demon. I am a demon.

Can she recognize me? Mama! It's me!

Then I feel the fire in my chest.

Then everything becomes cold.

20.

Am I writing this on paper? Or is paper just a remnant of my memory? Perhaps, paper is my memory.

I am writing this, speaking this, as a memory. My voice.

They have forgotten who I am.

But I remember who I was and what I am. They have made me their speaker, but inside, I am not their speaker,

I am myself.

I still fight the war against the invaders.

Perhaps, one day, my people, my mother, would accept me back.

Perhaps, one day, I would accept myself.

—fin—

Silver Wings

My mom gave me silver wings.

She actually gave me a silver suit, after she retired from her Spandex Club. That was like many years later after I turned 25 and she kept the suit in an airtight vacuum tube in a secret basement of our house.

You see, my mom was the legendary, all-powerful Silver Wing. Leader of the Spandex Club, a group of crime fighters who looked after our city and put thieves, arsonists, rapists and all sorts of low life in jail. Whenever there was a crime, the Spandex Club was there. I knew them, because they were my mom's friends and they often ate at our place, especially during Lunar New Year when mom got out her hotpot and everyone ate around the big table in our living room. They were my uncles and aunts, not related by blood, but they had watched me grow up. I loved their ang pows. The red envelopes came with money inside. Mom's house had pictures of them posing cheekily for the camera. Dad has always been the unofficial photographer. He loves cameras.

Mom was now happily growing succulents and tropical vegetables in our little greenhouse. She still had moments of anger when she watched the news or kept tabs on the police scanner in her study. Her knee injury and arthritis kept her out of the crime fighting, spandex wearing scene. Before she met dad and had me, she was this hotshot biologist and geneticist, working late nights in her lab at a prestigious university and developing a suit that produced bird wings.

After she got shot in the right knee by the Vile Rose, a villain who placed red roses in all her victims' mouths, mom basically said no more to the super hero life and spent many years feeling extremely unhappy while the Spandex Club, under the new leadership of Jinx, mom's best friend and occasional rival, flourished and kicked asses.

Me? I was a freaking *disappointment.*

I dropped out of university after the second year, dabbled around in odd jobs and finally settled in a career using my tits and ass. That's right. I was a porn actor, reporting at 8 in the morning and finishing at 8 at night, with my sweaty naked body in different angles and poses, while my male co-stars pumped away mechanically. It earned me my paycheck, minimal as it was . . . and mom's incandescent wrath.

"You should have stayed in university," mom said after I told her about my first role in a bsdm movie, a parody of some science fiction show. Her voice could have solidified water. Her eyes certainly paralyzed me to the spot. I was 5 years old all over again, standing in front of my crayons and a picture of my family. In the picture, I drew mom with huge black wings. I had just learnt what a dragon looked like in kindergarten. "You should have graduated by now."

"I have a paycheck," I stated stubbornly. It was true. I had my own apartment, in a less respectable area of our city, but still, *my own apartment.*

Mom put down the steel colander of half-washed bak choi with a solid thump on the kitchen counter. "Tell me you are still taking your MMA classes."

"Getting bruises every weekend," I hated to argue with her,

when she was obviously in the right. I hated having to defend myself all the goddamned time.

"Good," Mom picked up the colander again. It was a nice large one. Dad bought it for her last Christmas. *Trust Scandinavian products,* he whispered to me when he wrapped the colander in bright green and red paper that made my head swim with its sheer vibrancy. Last week, it was *Trust German precision.* "There are a lot of xiao ren in this city. Assholes and all."

I liked the MMA classes. It was all just body conditioning, reflexes and moves that would kill the next bloke who attacked you. I put them in good use. A couple of the directors of the said porn films were creeps. They had their heads stuffed in garbage bins the next morning. I didn't tell mom, because she would tell me about Steel Strong, who has arms of stainless steel. Her style was to go after men and pound the lights out of them.

It was after a strenuous session in Erotixxx Studios when I saw Tia come in with purple splotches on her face and arms. I was tired. The director was a perfectionist bastard. Many cuts, too many poses, and the vagina could only take that much lube and thrusting. I was glad to be out of the faux-king sized bed with creaky wooden legs and into the communal shower which, thankfully, the studio provided for their hardworking actors. I was drying my hair when Tia stripped off her white tee and jeans. I almost yelled.

"Don't tell me you fell down the stairs again," I winced at the bruises on her cheek and along her arms. They were purple shot through with a sickly green-yellow. I couldn't stop staring at them. That was the excuse she gave when I saw her last week. I knew she had an a-hole ex who liked their sex a bit too rough. She also said she bumped into corners or the edge of the table. But tables don't do that to a face.

This time, Tia just looked at me, like a cornered abused animal in a cage.

"Fuck, what did he do?" I shouted. Tia and me go a long way together. We started at the same time in this business and we had our fights and our tears. Tia recently became a bit of an Internet celeb by showing how fast she could orgasm.

"He hit me when I said no," Tia's voice was naturally husky. Now she sounded really broken. Beaten up inside and outside. Fuck. "I didn't want sex last night. He . . . he didn't like it."

"FUCK," I stood up, realized I was already standing up, and flung my wet towel into the laundry bin. Erotixxx was finicky to the point of draconian when it came to personal hygiene, since many of us were exchanging and dripping bodily fluids every-where. *"He's going to die."*

Tia grabbed my arm. She was shaking pretty hard. "No, please no, Sha, he will bloody kill you."

I hugged her, naked body and all. "You deserve better, so much better."

The bastard was predictable. I watched him return from the shit job he did at the mall: security guard. Typical dude with a uniform—power got into his head. Plus, he was just a massive asshole with abusive tendencies.

I whooped his ass when he got out of the lift, blocked his attempts at blocking me, and yes sir, I had my hair cut short (director had a hissy fit the next day). He couldn't grab my hair. Went for his privates, and when he keeled over, holding his much-abused balls, I slammed my heel into his neck. He dropped like a stone.

I dropped him at the doorstep of our precinct with a shiny red ribbon pinned on top of his head.

Tia was much happier and hugged me. She got her life back and threw all his things out. I soon started receiving private requests from the other girls *and* boys in the studio.

It was fun at first, beating up the lowlifes. Such an adrenaline rush! I could fight evil on my own.

But my body was mortal and prone to breakage. One of the idiots hit me hard in the ribs and I was out for a couple of weeks. I managed to stagger home, collapsing soon after. Mom was livid and concerned all at the same time. She made me delicious herbal tonics. She also lectured me about vigilantism, safety and protecting myself and all the things that came with crime-fighting. "You can't keep doing this on your own," she argued hotly.

Of course, I fought back. I always did. I said to her, in her face, that I could deal with all these lowlifes, all this evil, on my own. I didn't need her superhero powers. I had my fists, feet and my rage. "Aren't superheroes vigilantes too? You were a vigilante, mom!"

Mom didn't talk to me for two weeks. It was one of so many cold wars. Dad sent me reconciliatory messages and pictures of new pots and pans from his phone.

Then one day, out of the blue, she said, sounding tired via phone: "It's about time."

I gingerly limped my way—*another broken rib*—through Mom's things—her gardening tools, her boxes of stuff, and the stacks of biology 101 books—and cursed with feeling when my ribs rubbed against each other in an unpleasant way. Mom blithely weaved a path down our attic, out of place in her light blue sun dress and swirling dust motes. Boxes of Lunar New Year decorations dad didn't have the time (and didn't bother) to throw away, Christmas wrapping paper all in brittle and yellowing rolls, photo albums with a furry layer of dust. Some of them looked older than me. I spied a bicycle tucked all the way in one corner. Its sky blue paint was muted with age. The attic was filled with memories, some best forgotten.

I almost tripped over golden dragon streamers from last year's Lunar New Year. My right side immediately protested with throbbing.

Mom tapped a complex code on some touchpad panel (when did she install that in?) and the wall started to move. It slid open, a bit like some Starship Enterprise special effects—and I could smell something else: antiseptic. It reminded me of our toilets at home, where Mom would disinfect everything. I followed her in. It was as if I had stepped into her sanctum, her special place—a place I didn't know existed. It was all panels and computer screens right smack in the middle of the room . . . lab? There was a huge glass cylindrical tank, a bit like the fish tank we saw at SeaWorld. In the middle of the tank, suspended in mid-air, was a silver one-piece swimsuit. Conservative, a bit like mom. Tasteful, again, like mom.

Mom tapped more complex codes on the panel next to the tank. The glass door hissed open. With an almost reverential manner, she reached out and picked the silver swim suit just like that. It was hanging by some force-field. *Force-field? What the hell.*

"We are of the same size," mom's voice was soft. "The nano-zoids make the suit flexible and stretchable." She held it out to me, expecting me to hold it.

"Mom, I can fight evil on my own," I said, staring at the suit. Why was I so hesitant? It was just a suit, for crying out loud.

"You can't keep going after all these men," Mom said. "Not with my help. I am not forcing you to choose. I just wanted to give you another option."

My inner voice screamed *I can do it my own!* but my body had other ideas. I touched the suit, after inhaling a lungful of air. *Breathe, Sha, breathe.* It felt like nylon, with a silky texture. I expected it to be plastic-y, but it was warm on my skin.

When mom wore it, it had large white wings that shone like the angel on our Christmas tree. "On silver wings I rise!" was her battle-cry. The Spandex Club talked about it all the time, over their mahjong sessions and hotpot steam rising from boiling vegetable broth. I often listened in, in the usual way of trying hard not to look as if I were listening in, to their gossip. Auntie Jinx hated the battle-cry and wanted mom to change it. Besides, would villains care about posturing and stupid speeches ? I also knew Crow Man had a thing for mom and still did, in his own awkward way. He often bought her flowers for her birthday.

Mom's wings were fluffy, like a swan's outspread wings. I hated swans. They bite. She beat down criminals with those wings. She didn't have superpowers, like Steel Strong, Crow Man or even Emerald Light—she only had her wits, her reflexes and her suit.

She did it like me. *She did it on her own.* I suddenly remembered something. Me learning how to ride the bicycle when I was four and pouting "I do it my own!" while pushing Mom's hands away. Mom just stood there, looking sad and happy at the same time. She was so much younger then.

Mom wanted me to wear the suit in front of her. I think she was almost bursting with pride. Suddenly I was shy. Me, who would easily peel off her clothes and fuck a dude for the camera—shy. For crying out loud. I asked her to wait outside so that I could try the suit on. Mom rolled her eyes and laughed, her eyes twinkling. I realized her hair was all silver now, edged with hints of black.

The suit was surprisingly easy to wear. It was in some ways like a one piece swimsuit. I hadn't worn one since I was nine. Mom was right: the whatever nanozoids made it very flexible. The suit *fit*. Perfectly. No boob spillage. No bit of fat showing. It was perfect. For a moment, I stood in the middle of mom's secret hangout, wearing her suit. My head felt light. My heart pounded.

My wings. Mom didn't tell me what to do about the wings part. Do I just imagine them to be? And what kind of wings should I have? I was not a swan.

Hawk. Falcon. I liked birds of prey. Raptors. I had pictures of eagles and hawks pasted all over the wall. I was the weird kid who loved birds in middle and high school. The image of a peregrine falcon flashed through my mind. The suit tightened slightly and I could feel my shoulder-blades taking a life of their own. It was just the suit's little critters responding to my thought. There was no turning back now.

A rustle, a stab of pain through my shoulder-blades, and wings sprouted from my back. There was a rush of wind and me going "FUCK" when I felt myself being lifted upwards. I fought to remain on earth. Another "FUCK" and I landed clumsily on my feet. I saw my reflection in the panel opposite the glass tank: I had wings. Falcon wings. They were brown, with highlights of gold. As I watched, spellbound, the wings twitched and took on a silver sheen.

Mom came in at that exact moment and then we were laughing, crying and holding each other all at once. She stood back after and smiled. "Oh wow," she said. I wiped off the tears from my own eyes. I was not a disappointment to her. I didn't draw those dragon wings on her. I didn't push her away.

That evening, she had the Spandex Club over for an impromptu celebratory dinner. Hotpot as usual, with the platters of succulent shellfish, fish slices, bak choi, fish balls and shabu-shabu meat from the nearby Asian grocery shop. She introduced me as the new Silver Wing. The Spandex Club nodded sagely and each of them hugged me. They were my uncles and aunts. Auntie Jinx wiped away a tear and gave me a box of durian praline chocolates all the way from Singapore. Dad took pictures. We had wefies. Then we ate our dinner.

Later that evening, I stood at the roof top of one of the buildings, accompanied by Steel Strong's daughter, Dagger. My wings hung behind me. I felt their weight. I felt Mom's legacy.

"Let's kick some ass," Dagger smiled. She had silver arms like her mom's and a deliciously wicked laugh. I wanted to kiss her hard on the lips. She was gorgeous. She wore a different costume from her mom's: all yellow, not like a sunflower, but the sun itself. I should ask her out.

Earlier, I asked her why she became Dagger and she shrugged, grinning. "Ain't superhuman all the time. I am only mortal. Can't do it on my own forever."

"I said the same thing too," I said

"There you go," Dagger smiled.

I listened to the city sounds, the noises that formed the heartbeat of the city. I thought about Tia and thousands of women like her. My ribs were still sore, but they would heal. I still had to turn up for the "Hot Girls Making Out" shoot tomorrow. A bitch still had to eat and pay her rent. *I can do this on my own.* For now, these would have to wait. Somewhere, there was the sound of glass shattering. Closer, I heard a couple arguing over steaks being overdone. She blamed their old grill. He yelled at her about the sauce gone bitter. A sound followed, a slap on skin. The woman sobbing.

Red-hot anger spiked. My wings flared. I focused on the on-going argument, on the sound of sobbing.

"Yes," I nodded. "Let's kick some."

Dagger took the first leap out, vaulting over the roof-tops like a parkour champion. Her yellow form flickered like a living flame as she darted from roof to roof, jumping across the gaps as if she were born to do this. I just had to take my first step. What was stopping me? Fear? Tia's face swam before me. The sound of the woman sobbing reverberated in my mind. *Me pouting and pushing Mom away.* My fists clenched. My wings stiffened before spreading fully. The feathers were mercury silver edged with the diffuse gold of the city lights.

The wings will listen to you, Mom said during the hotpot dinner, her chopsticks poised above her bowl of food. You are the wings. Will yourself to fly. Will yourself to soar. You are the Silver

Wing, Li Shan. She hadn't used my name for a while now. The steam from the boiling vegetable broth looked like joss smoke drifting skywards.

Dagger—*real name: Nala*—was already at the end of the street. She pumped her fist, once, twice. It was now or never.

How did you fight, Mom? With fists and feet? With brains and wits?

Like me.

How did you fight?

Like me.

How *do* you fight?

Like me.

How do *I* fight?

Nala pumped her fist impatiently.

I am the Silver Wing now. I will fight with brains and wits, fists and feet. I can do this on my own. I can do this. With silver wings, I rose.

I cried the cry of a hunting falcon.

The night was mine. The city embraced me with its sounds and colors.

—fin—

Garra Rufa

The first time she saw garra rufa she was five months pregnant with Anna. Cooped up at home, she was dying to go out, breathe some fresh air and just be. So Max decided to take her to a farmers' market. Her belly was taut and tight as if someone had stuffed a basketball up her dress. Yet she felt as light as a balloon, flitting from one stall to another, tasting the samples and buying bags of nuts so that she could nibble on, because she needed to eat all the time. Then she saw the small shop, not even a proper spa, with the tanks of fish. She had heard from Ying how marvelous these fish were.

"Can I?" she asked Max. The bored shop owner palmed their ten dollars. She had to wash her feet. The water was cold, jotting her awake. The filters in the tank bubbled. There was a faint smell of *fish* in the air. The tanks reminded her of her grandfather's fish farm.

The fish looked like carp and were half the length of her middle finger, and just as slim. They darted about in silver spurts. Up close, as she slipped her feet into the lukewarm water, they began circling her toes, as if they were sizing her up. The first few nibbles, of tiny teeth tickling skin, made her laugh. The baby kicked when she did. What a grumpy baby, she thought, as her right foot was covered with a swirling mass of fish.

Max looked downright unhappy. He thought the whole skin-eating fish thing was nonsense. What an idiot, she thought further.

Then later in the night, when they went back home, she began to bleed. It was placenta previa, according to the medical doctor attending her at the emergency room. Max's look was *serve-you-right* and *I-told-you-so*. She was too tired to argue with him when he was in this sort of mood.

The second time she saw garra rufa she had to take over Han's failing spa shop. Anna clung to her legs when she walked up and down the shop which had the faint smell of fish. The fish-eating-dead-skin business was a bandwagon everybody under the hot Singaporean sun wanted to jump on, just like bubble tea. Shops popped up and then died as the clueless well-meaning owners failed to comprehend the rearing of fish and the running of a business. Han practically ran the business to the ground. The tanks were green and filthy. The filters didn't—couldn't—work. Even the fake green plants—to make the shop look more tropical—failed. They now gathered dust and cobwebs where the only industrious ones were the spiders in the shop catching flies.

"You have experience with fish," Han looked so happy, so *relieved*. She smiled wanly. Just because she spent all her June holidays helping grandfather at his fish farm didn't make her an instant fish expert. These were fish from the Middle East. Grandfather's business dealt with fish for the wealthy: koi and arowana.

"Did you check the temperature?" she pretended to roll out all the right questions. "Did you change the filters?"

Of course, Max complained as usual. She divorced him the next year, when Anna turned seven.

The third time she saw garra rufa she had two spas with proper masseuses and well-filtered tanks filled with the fish. The fish had consumed her life. She suddenly became familiar with garra rufa, the fish from Turkey. They were known to eat dead skin, cure psoriasis and were known as doctor fish. Of course, they were not truly doctors. Garra rufa only ate dead skin when food was scarce. They were more like algae feeders. She fed them specialized food.

"You are so lucky," Han praised her.

She didn't tell Han and Ying that she dreamed of garra rufa nightly. They swam in her subconscious, darting in and out of the ornamental fish tank grass. In the dreams, they were numerous and bright as stars. They would swirl about her, whispering to her in their fish voices. She would spin and spin while they spiraled up in the night sky of her dreams, scattering into shimmering silver-gold constellations. She would sing in the dreams, something she had stopped doing so when she was awake and caring for Anna, for the shops, for herself and for ... She had stopped singing when grandfather's fish farm closed down because the government decided to take over since land was so scarce in Singapore. When she passed the place where the huge farm once stood weeds sprouted from the ground and ferns burst out in clusters on the roofs that covered the nursery for the fish fry. The land had lain empty for years now. State property, the signboard stated sternly.

She had tried to look for grandfather's papers. Did his title deed expire? Where did he put his papers? Grandmother only shook her head. This was the same woman who hid all her savings in a metal biscuit tin.

The fourth time she saw garra rufa she was in one of her dreams, only that she had become one of them, a garra rufa female. Fully-grown, they looked like miniature dark carp the length of her hand. Not as pretty as grandfather's prized koi, but just as elegant and inscrutable. She darted in and out of the grass with the rest of the school, listening only to her instincts. There was lack of food. The algae was almost gone. She was hungry. She needed to feed.

Anna's face pressed against the fish tank. Food, she swam frantically, food food food give me food. Her daughter's face scrunched up, before laughing. Someone—the hand!—sprinkled flakes. She shot up, gobbling up the food.

She woke up with her heart pounding. The air conditioning unit above her head dripped cold water. She had to get it fixed. She was glad to see her hands and feet.

The fifth time she saw garra rufa she slapped the title deed onto the counter of the officer in front of her. He had a picture of garra rufa as wallpaper on his computer. They looked happy, these garra rufa, in their little controlled environment. She told the officer that the land was still hers, her family's and she had the right to get it back from the government.

Max called her later and remarked that she was going mad. She blocked his call. The damn idiot had been pestering her since the divorce. He just didn't know when to give up. Of course, she won the custody of Anna. Damn idiot didn't lift a finger to help through these years. He fainted when she strained to give birth. What a useless man, always sullen and never saying a positive word. All the money she used to build the spas up was hers. Now that she was rich he was trying to worm his way back to her life.

The sixth time she saw garra rufa she was in the tank. She had stripped naked, like Godiva. She stepped into the tank, the luke-warm water slowly inching up her thighs. The filters bubbled. She loved the smell of fish. The moment she sat down in the tank the cameras started snapping. Her campaign had to work. The media loved her. She was the garra rufa lady and she was drawing in the media circle like moths to an open raging fire.

She just wanted her land back.

She leant back, feeling the water envelop her. Her pubic hair floated like underwater moss. As she waited for the fish to swarm around her, she was reminded of a picture she had seen. Ophelia floating down the stream. Dying with flowers about her, all dreamy and gorgeous. She was turning into a mermaid, a garra rufa.

Tiny mouths began nibbling quickly at her skin. She sighed, her mouth parting open, only that she gave forth a stream of bubbles. She felt their love, their hunger criss-crossing her body. Better than a lover's, any lover's—and so gentle, so insistent, so pure.

Max's face ghost-white against the tank, his fists thumping the tank. She couldn't hear him. She was becoming garra rufa. Her dead skin was being stripped away, removed. The fish were changing her. She was changing. She was breaking up into a school of star-bright, star-quick fish, and she was one of the fish heading towards the sky, like fireflies in grandfather's fish farm. There wasn't any light at night. The stars were bright. The fire-lights were moving stars. She was becoming as light as a balloon. Somewhere, grandfather waved.

Anna's face crying against the tank, her hands slapping the tank as if it was a hateful thing.

The seventh time she saw garra rufa she saw them in the tank before her, dark shapes that moved like stars. She rested her hand on her swollen belly. The shop smelled of fish. The shop owner looked bored. There hadn't been any customers, except for a couple of aunties who giggled with their feet in the water. Max stared at her, wondering why she had suddenly stopped for seven minutes, looking into empty air. He was genuinely concerned. Perhaps the farmers' market was a bad idea.

"Come, let's sit down and have a drink," she smiled and led him away. "It's hot and I need to rest."

"Good idea," Max was glad she took his advice to rest.

She smiled once more, sipping her water. She had plans for grandfather's fish farm.

—fin—

Qi Xi

you should fly
fragile bones
and your heart
beat
beat
beat
your gilded cage

cannot
hold you

the stars call your name
and the nebulas
are your skies
the Pleiades
your home

somewhere,
they meet, hand in hand,
the bridge of your kin

a red wedding string
joining generation
after generation

you should fly
fragile bones

you should fly
fragile bones

and your heart
beat the song
of
starry hope

stay strong,
dear heart,
stay strong.

The Bridge

Xe often hears about the bridge that
–links–

one world to another,
a bridge

of hope that
gives xer People visions of the future.

Xe is young and xer teeth are
not as sharp as xer siblings,
nor as old and ancient as xer parents
who hunt in the darkest layers of the currents,
catching fish and other things
that skitter in the night,
flashes of starlight silver
easily frightened and herded by song.

Xer People are singers,
their songs of water, of diving and of fierce joy
in hunting, in children, in sleeping curled
while the water turns
cold, cold, cold.

The stories are about the bridge,
that in times of pain,
the blood kin moves from one world to another,
bringing all their hopes to
a new world
with welcome water, food, and joy.

"What are they like?" xe often asks,
and xer mother laughs deep, like the moving of the land
beneath the water.

            "Our kin looks like us, breathes like us, hunts like us,
                                only their words are different,
                    but we only have trust and kindness to share."

Then the deaths happen,
People floating up, cut, slashed, dead.

The water tastes of death
                of unspoken pain and of deep sorrow so strong,
                    it is hard to swim in it, breathe in it, hunt in it.

"We have to go," father says
and xis eyes are sad like deep, deep night
when the warm-blooded ones howl in the distance,
and their songs are of their people's joy and pain.

Xe often hears about the bridge that
                        –links–

                                one world to another.

                And the bridge is dark and cold and forbidding,
                            with the coldness of not-love
                                and not-kindness.

Xe pauses, stares up at xer kin,
xer sisters and brothers,
xer parents, so strong and so tired.

    "Is this the bridge where we swim to meet our cousins?
        Where we are welcomed, and we can stay?"

So they take the journey,
through the bridge,
where the monsters have sharp teeth,
                              and hungrier stomachs,
                         and eyes that shine like greed.

Father dies, defending them from a demon maw,
            Mother protects, but even then, xer body
                 floats up, up, up and xer siblings
                         cry, cry, cry.

At last, they reach the end of the bridge,
orphans,
                                   homeless, family-less.
                    Alone.

Xe swims forward, xer fins sore,
and xer body faint from lack of food,
and everything seems against xer.

            In the distance, xe sees the shapes,
                 like xers, like xer siblings,
                 and perhaps there is hope.
                         Xe sings, and listens for the reply.

            Silence.

Then, the song comes back,
a little different,
but the feelings are the same.

            Xe knows xe is home.

                    —fin—

The Land

Saints And Bodhisattvas

Where the straits interlaced each other with the confluences of currents and trade routes was the famed Golden Chersonese, a beacon of light, the center of all wealth and riches. Saints and bodhisattvas met there, allies in the inter-exchange of spirituality and learning. You would find your path there, they said. You would never hunger nor would you thirst. Bewitching creatures lurked in the Golden Chersonese, fantastic animals that populated your mind's bestiary. Birds of paradise with tails that flamed like the sun, dragons with large flickering tongues and poisonous saliva, and large cats that roared and founded a city. It lured many explorers, sailors of the sea and wind. It lured me.

I was born in the middle, a straddler between two worlds, one of the sea and one of solid land. The midwife laughed and said I was destined to ride the waves, breathing both ocean air and the sap of sea almond and angsana trees easily. Ibu was perturbed by the midwife's words, but she only held me, so she said, trying to protect me from the elements. I was in the middle, where the currents of life swirled like whirlpools forming at the wake of ships. At two, I was already swimming. At four, I stood at the prow of a skiff, the sea breeze on my face, the sea singing in my veins. At ten, I joined my father in his travels. I remembered soaring sun-baked stupas, the Sanskrit and Pali of saffron-robed monks, and the solemn tolling of gereja bells on Formosa's hill. I remembered the fragrance of spices and sandalwood wafting through the narrow sun-baked streets of Melaka, the cries of the vendors hawking their wares.

When I turned eighteen, I was given my own perahu. Rare for a girl, but I was never a girl, never a boy either. I wore a lacy kebaya at home, a simple chinon and baggy trousers at sea. My hair was bound tight. I swung on ropes, unencumbered by loose strands of hair. My right hand held a dao, a gift from a friend whom I saved. His ship burned, his cargo gone, but he lived. He was grateful to be alive. I was a saint for saving him.

I fought with his dao, now my dao. With it, I explored the Golden Chersonese.

Then, she came into my life like a bodhisattva.

My men were loudly discussing the merits of cooking while they repaired my ship. Away from home, they longed for their homes so they distracted themselves with repair work. Sleek, sharp of prow, my ship cut through the sea like a kris. Yet it was not invincible against the forces of nature. Wood wore down easily, got chipped and sometimes dented. The underside of the ship had to be scraped thoroughly. Months at sea meant abundant growth of sea life. The sharp edges of the shells on the ship's sides hurt our exposed skin.

They joked about making seafood kari with the mussels as they removed them. On lean days we often picked them off the sides of the ship and ate them boiled in coconut water. I never liked them. I craved my mother's ulam. I missed the cleansing taste of the finely-chopped herbs and the bitterness of the fried shallots. But to play along, I laughed with them, like the way my father had taught me. In their eyes, I was the towkay's son.

The last raid saw our rival, another band of lanun, trying to escape. In their panic, they rammed the prow of their perahu into the side of my ship. The sound of it made me sick to the stomach. It reminded me of breaking bones. We were lucky water didn't seep in. We limped into our port, our lives and cargo intact. I was livid. We would have to spend the whole month repairing the ship and miss a season of plying the sea before the torrential rains returned. I hated returning to port and having to wait the rains out. For the repairs, I traded in a new chest of precious Chinese silk in exchange for tools and timber. I had intended the chest to be sold to a buyer. It felt like a bad start to the season.

Around this time, the dry season was nearing its end, ready to go but unwilling to leave. The land was parched, the grass a brittle brown, and the wind hot against my cheeks. It blew in gusts, stirring up puffs of dust from the ground. A large desiccated spider tumbled across my sandaled feet. The withdrawing tide exposed the seabed rippling with life. Tiny fish darted in the pools of clear water. Crabs waved their pincer claws. I leaned back into the warm sand, my arm across my eyes, glad for some respite. I only wanted the repairs done as soon as possible. The heat lulled me into a light nap.

I heard someone walking towards me, footsteps crunching on the sand. I glimpsed beaded slippers with glittering beads of vivid red and green. Beaded slippers? I raised my face then to the glare of the afternoon sun. She stood before me, imperious, the sunlight outlining a slim figure clothed in a vivid sea-green kebaya and red sarong. Young nonyas were usually accompanied by a stern matronly chaperone when they left their house, if they ever left it at all. They led sheltered lives. What a rare occurrence indeed.

"You must be the captain of the *Sri Matahari*," the voice was young and confident, clear with precise pronunciation of the patois spoken in our parts of the Golden Chersonese. I got up quickly, dusting my chinon trousers as I surveyed the girl in front of me.

Her hair was a light brown. Under the sun, the strands shimmered gold. Her skin was the color of my own: the color of a Peranakan child—olive skin with subtle shades of perang. Her dark eyes were large and bright with a lively intelligence. Portuguese Kristang, then. There was a large population of them in this part of Melaka. They were mostly fishermen. The wealthier ones ran shipping consortiums.

"I am," I said briskly.

"I have a request ... a job for you," the young woman continued without any introduction. "I will pay you."

I smiled wryly. "I won't agree to any request without knowing the name of my potential hirer."

Her full lips twitched. She must have pouted a lot as a child. She schooled her irritation with a smile too. "I am Maria."

"What can I do for you, Maria?" I stifled my own chuckle. She must have thought I was a man.

She leaned forward suddenly, her manner at once shy and conspiring. Something flashed bright at her neck. A silver necklace. "I want you to kill a man."

"Kill a man?"

I raised an eyebrow. I had encountered such requests before and twice I refused them very politely. I wasn't an assassin.

"Captain Neo," Maria said severely.

"So you do know my name. Back to my question: Kill a man?"

"Not so loud!" the young woman snorted. My first mate, Halim, looked up sharply. He was always alert and quick to respond. That was why he was my father's first mate and now mine. Only he knew who I actually was.

"I am not a killer," I shook my head.

"You are lanun. Lanun kill people," Maria pushed on. I frowned. I was beginning to dislike her attitude. I wanted her to go away. "You are not averse to killing."

"You must have mistaken me for something I am not. I am just a simple trader." I said very mildly. My men knew that particular tone very well. Suddenly, all repair work stopped and the men stood up, very slowly, with hands on their parangs and kris knives, glaring darkly at her. "You have such a low opinion of us. We are not the ruffians you think we are."

"Ai meu Deus!" Maria said angrily. She had noticed their reaction. She was no fool.

"I know that expression, senhora. You don't have to swear."

"I would like you to hunt down the man who killed my father," Maria whispered, her voice harsh, almost guttural. Her eyes were wet with unshed tears and she clearly hated showing that weakness in front of me and my men. "I know who and what you really are. *Please help me.*"

Her voice tugged at something in me. Loss. Pain. Despair. I thought of my father, already several years dead. He died when I was twenty, a victim of the prolonged coughing sickness.

"*Please.* Que os santos te abençoem."

May the saints bless you. I knew the phrase. All the captains who plied the Golden Chersonese learned the two or three languages spoken at the major and minor ports, beside the "port tongue" which was a mixture of all the languages together. I glanced at the silver necklace on her neck. It was a small crucifix. Serani. Most of the Portuguese Kristang were called Serani by the rest.

Against my better judgment, I nodded.

Her full name was Maria Fernandes.

Once she was perceived as non-threatening, my men went back to repairing the ship, their voices loud enough to be heard from the deck where I invited Maria for freshly brewed Ceylon tea. I did so, because it was the right way to show hospitality to guests, and because this was the way my father had taught me. It was also a good way to gauge my guest face to face, over tea and preserved sweetmeats from my own personal store.

Maria took off her slippers to walk up the wooden plank, even mincing daintily across without losing her balance. She politely declined my helping hand to step into the ship. Her sarong restricted her movements, yet she moved quickly and with grace. Soon, she sat, legs tucked under her, while I poured the tea into delicate porcelain cups. They were the craze at the moment, all the way from China. She nibbled on the sweetmeats, complimenting the taste of the sugared dry hawthorn. I sipped my tea, wondering who she really was, where her family lived.

"I am an orphan," she said without being prompted. "If you

are curious as I think you are. I was adopted by a Peranakan family ... But I left on amiable terms. This kebaya and sarong ... they belong to a friend who took me in out of pity." She lapsed into silence, staring into the sea. Heat shimmered over the horizon. The sky was a clear blue.

"Ah, I see," I said. "How will you pay me? This is a business transaction."

She looked up, her eyes wide, her nostrils flaring. I realized she was afraid. "I will ... pay you once the deed is done. At the meantime, please grant me permission to work onboard your ship."

"This is still very vague, Maria. I can't work on the basis of empty terms. My men need payment. Let me remind you that we are all rough people," I shook my head. "We are all used to rough and hard work."

Maria stared hard at me. "I have heard rumors about you, that you are actually a woman in disguise. I can work just as hard as a man."

"What if I am?" I challenged back, suddenly angry at the intrusion of my privacy. Rumors were often spread by jealous gossip and idle chatter. "Can you handle a weapon? Will you faint at the sight of blood?"

"NO!" her shout startled me with its sheer vehemence. "I am not some fragile flower! If it's handling weapons you want, I can do it. Teach me!" She spat the words out as if they bothered her.

"Well, then," I said finally. "My ship's still being repaired. We can't leave immediately."

"I can wait," Maria pouted. "Even if it means a month."

Halim chose this time to pop up, peering straight into the

ship at us. He was a wiry man, built for the sea. Age had grizzled his temples, but his eyes were still sharp, his tongue even sharper. I saw him as a father of sorts, a replacement for my own. He wore his customary dark sarong and left his torso bare. His family kris hung by his side. "Adakah semua dalam keadaan yang baik?" he asked, glancing at Maria sternly. Maria glared back, unafraid.

"We are well," I smiled, waving him away. "Don't worry."

My first mate nodded curtly and ducked back out into the afternoon sun, shouting orders to the crew to stop lazing around. Maria left her tea untouched. "I have no family left," she said.

"We will talk more tomorrow," I said, suddenly tired. Maria's presence had stirred emotions I'd thought were gone. I missed my family.

⁂

I woke up from a dream where my mother was making sambal with the batu giling. Her strong hands rolled the stone cylindrical pestle across the large mortar board. I could hear the stone grinding against the chilli and herbs. Somewhere, someone was singing. The smell of the chopped galangal and chilli being mixed intoxicated me. My heart ached with longing. I opened my mouth to say something to my ibu . . . only to peer up, sore and ill-rested, at the ceiling of my cabin.

I found Maria waiting for me at the bottom of the ship. It was barely morning yet. The tide had rolled in and the hint of rain was in the air. The men slept in, wrapped in their sarongs. Only Halim seemed awake. He was idly fishing, but I knew he was also alert and listening for any sign of trouble.

She had not slept. She was still wearing her kebaya and was wrapped in a tattered shawl. I glanced down at her feet. Bare. The beaded slippers were gone.

"Are you comfortable?" I asked. Maria smiled wanly at me. "We walk barefoot on the ship. Are you sure you don't need protection for your feet?" My own were callused from years on board ships.

She only nodded. The sky was beginning to lighten. A silver of golden orange peered over the east. Was Maria the kind to bolt? Time to seal the agreement. I spat into my right hand and extended it to Maria. Without hesitation, she spat into her right palm and then pressed it against mine. She didn't even flinch.

"Your life is now mine and my life is now yours," I intoned the formal phrase used amongst people of our particular trade. "You share your food with us and we share our food with you. We eat the same food. We breathe the same air. The sea protects you and me."

"Amém," Maria said, crossing herself. My lips quirked. I decided I was going to like her.

"Let's break fast," I walked towards Halim who had started a fire to grill the ikan kuning he'd caught. "And let us get you something to wear. That finery has to go."

"Please let me keep the kebaya," Maria hurried to join me. "I want to remember something from my former life."

"Of course," I answered coolly. The cooking fish smelled delicious.

We found headgear, a plain grey chinon and dark green trousers for Maria. The headgear came from Halim's own pile of clothing, the chinon and trousers from my chest since we shared a similar body type. Divested of her kebaya and sarong, Maria looked like a boy in her new clothes, her hair tied up into a tight bun and hidden under the headgear. She wore no weapon yet. Her necklace still hung on her neck.

She ate with what seemed like a healthy appetite, picking the flesh off the fish bone with her fingers and chewing the whole fish head before chasing it down with more Ceylon tea.

"The ship's not ready yet," Halim reported. "We need one day more."

"Our men are hardworking," I said. My first mate grinned, a flash of white teeth.

"They are motivated by the sea," he said, before leaning closer, darting a quick look at Maria who remained ignored by the rest of the men who swarmed over the ship. "You trust *her*?"

"Hers is a blood feud. She seeks revenge."

"Keep an eye on her, kapitan. I would rather have her off the ship."

"She has no family."

Halim snorted. "That's the reason given by half of our men. And . . . she's . . . you know . . . a woman . . . " He let the sentence trail into silence.

"You said that about me a long time ago."

"You are our towkay's child."

"Son. Our towkay's *son*."

Halim's face reddened. "Kapitan, you proved yourself on the

sea. Her? I am not sure, though I have heard that there are women on the other ships too, just as fierce and bloodthirsty as men."

"Let her go clean the ship's deck first," I said finally, wrapping my headgear around my head. "That's her first test."

By mid-day, Maria hung around like a bedraggled ghost. The ship floor was scrubbed but she was thorough.

"Not bad," Halim said, sounding unconvinced.

"Let her mend the sails," I said.

By evening, she sat, looking pale. The sails were mended, the tears neatly sewn. She managed to get the tools from the men who treated her as some sort of novelty. Halim made seafood kari, the spices courtesy from our own supplies, the fish and shrimp netted from the day's catch. Maria received her coconut husk-bowl of kari and retreated to the prow of the ship where she ate alone.

"Now let us see if she decides to stay," I nibbled at my own food.

I was woken up by the sound of splashing water and the smell of cooking fire. I peered out from my cabin. Maria was boiling water in the tin kettle. Fish was already cooking on wooden skewers she picked from the fallen twigs beneath the portia trees. She had caught enough for all of us.

I smiled.

Sri Matahari cut through the water, as if relieved to be released from confinement. Her sails caught the wind full. I heard them humming their familiar song. Around me, the men went about their usual duties, checking the ropes, the hooks and sharpening their weapons. Halim stood at the lookout, his eyes watching everything. Our pilot, Abdullah, steered the rudder. He had an intuitive touch when it came to guiding the ship.

"Maria!" I barked.

She ran up quickly. Her eyes sparkled. I could feel her excitement. So far she had shown no seasickness. She didn't seem to mind the sea. Perhaps, somewhere in her blood, there was sea water.

"Where does the murderer of your father live?" I asked.

"Temasek," she replied quickly, her voice cold. "He lives on Temasek."

✺

While *Sri Matahari* sailed, I taught Maria basic weapon drills. I couldn't possibly teach her all the things I knew. Instead, I chose one weapon and stuck to it. Maria handled the dagger easily. Block, attack, strike. Block, attack, strike. I knew the men watched the practice from the corner of their eyes, still painfully polite and reluctant to engage her with their activities.

"You need to be more aggressive," I pushed her. "Attack me. The people you meet later will not be nice nor will they be gentle."

Maria gritted her teeth. She had stopped pouting. In fact, I had not seen her pout since she came aboard. She came at me, her guard open. I stepped aside and twisted her arm. She struggled.

"Again," I said. I released her. She didn't rub her arm. Instead, she inhaled deeply, closing her eyes, before opening them again. She rushed, I evaded, only to have her side-step me. Her foot caught me off-balance. I tripped and stumbled. The men chuckled.

She reached down to help me up. Her grip was strong. I got to my feet. I could smell Maria. She smelled of spices and sweat. Her hair oil was not unpleasant, her body soft and warm. I felt my body respond, a flush of moist heat between my legs. The response surprised me. I had never felt like this before.

Before I could speak, she had placed her dagger onto my bare neck. I felt the cold edge press gently against the skin. "Surprise," she whispered in my ear. "*You have thick soles. I think you need shoes.*" She smirked.

"Beginner's luck," I pulled away, scowling at her. "Well done and *thank you, no, I don't.*"

Halim sighted the ship from a distance.

We were nearing Temasek, having navigated the complex network of small islands and sandy shoals surrounding the island. Maria had spent the week on the ship learning how to steer the rudder, wrestle and hone her fighting skills, and scrub the deck with coconut-husk bristles. The week had passed uneventfully. The season had only begun. Most ships would only emerge from their hide-outs and ports once the merchant ships arrived. The ones plying the straits now were either fishermen or ... people like us.

I had grown used to watching Maria prepare hot water and food every morning. I ... grappled with the surge of emotions and physical sensations whenever I saw her. I dreaded and craved standing next to her. She was the saint I couldn't bear to touch, a bodhisattva so holy I felt guilty for even walking close to her. An exquisite and rare beautiful bird-of-paradise. Yet, she saw me as her captain and the person whom she had hired to kill her father's murderer. The voice of reason in me warned me to stay far away from her and maintain an air of business. I had never had a woman on board my ship. Halim was right. It stirred up *things* in me.

The men were not immune either. One by one, they started to drift close to her, so that they could catch a glimpse of her before scuttling away with their dignity intact. A couple of them tried to share food with her. When she washed herself with the clean water we stored in barrels, everyone pretended not to see. We draped a sheet across her part of the ship to cordon off the area. Yet, she didn't seem interested in any of the men. She treated them like older brothers. Strange and distant older brothers.

Kill the murderer, get my payment, and we would be rid of her. These thoughts filled my head.

Where would she go once the deed was done?

"Perahu!" Halim shouted.

It slid in confidently, like a hunting shark lured by blood and the prospect of a meal. The perahu was of the same make as *Sri Matahari*. Its sails were angled sharply. The captain was banking on speed. There were lanun who prided themselves on their attack skills. Many were hit-and-run experts: attack their opponent or merchant, take what they needed, kill everyone aboard. I had seen ships adrift at sea, the crew dead and the cargo stolen. Most of the time, we just sailed past and offered a prayer.

What else could we do?

There were ten figures standing at the side of the ship, their weapons drawn. They were ready to board. Their pilot was steering the perahu so that it was heading at us directly. They were ready to board and kill. Abdullah yanked at the rudder and *Sri Matahari* moved, pulling away. It was our own tactic, to draw the enemy into a circling dance. "Let them give chase," I said, my heart pounding. I relished the taste of the hunt. My blood was singing in my veins. Beside me, Maria swallowed convulsively. Her eyes widened.

The lanun drew close, enough to see their features. Their faces showed a range of colors: perang and putih. There were three Dutch men among them. Some of the Dutch decided to stay after incursions into the area. Most had moved to Batavia where I heard they wreaked havoc and were terrible masters. They had fought with the Portuguese for territory: local rulers used them as pawns in their own bid for power. These Dutch men looked battle-hardened, their skin thick and leathery, their eyes fierce. They wore the same clothing with the rest. They had thrown in their lot with these lanun.

"Short sabers," Halim muttered darkly. "Probably stolen." He hated the Dutch.

Maria gripped her dagger with a wild look on her face. She seemed to have seen something . . . someone on the ship.

"What's wrong, Maria?" I said.

"It's *him*. I recognize him. He's there on the ship!" Her voice trembled, halfway between fear and exhilaration.

"Who's he?" I growled.

"My father's killer. One of the white men! There, look, he's wearing headgear!"

I saw him. He was a middle-aged man with white hair and grizzled face. Tall and lanky, he leaned heavily to his left. Old injury?

"Are you sure?" Halim snapped.

"Yes!" Maria shivered. "Yes!"

"You ready?" I asked her. "Are you sure?" I repeated Halim's question.

"Yes, I am."

"Abdullah, we are going in," I shouted.

Abdullah needed no further instruction. *Sri Matahari* began her attack run.

۞

"He killed your father?" I whispered.

"Yes, he did. They fought over something a long time ago. They were ... friends. He killed papa. He killed him and Mama pined to her death. I saw her die. I was only ten. *Ten.* I want to kill him for what he did to Papa and Mama. He destroyed my family!" Maria's knuckles were white, her breathing shallow. Her eyes, though, blazed with hatred.

"Today you get to kill him and avenge them," I said.

We drew close enough to board. The lanun yelled curses at us. My men hurled the boarding hooks.

With a laugh, I leaped across, my dao aimed at the captain of the ship.

He was an old man, even older than Halim but he fought harder than a cornered harimau. Still, I managed to subdue him, kicking him hard in the ribs. He fell hard backwards, his head hitting the boards. Dark blood seeped beneath the head. His men roared, having witnessed the death of their captain ... They were going to fight even more viciously now.

In the tumult of combat, I didn't see Maria. Everybody was busy killing or not getting themselves killed.

The chaos parted, to reveal Maria confronting the Dutchman who killed her father. Her eyes screamed death. She yelled a stream of Portuguese words so obscure I didn't understand most of them. Only "death" and "go to hell" made sense.

The man seemed to freeze, as if he recognized her, before he launched into a series of slashing cuts to drive her off. He wanted to kill her.

Maria ducked, dodging the saber. The silver necklace swung, catching the light of the sun. Then my line of vision was hindered by a tumbling mess of wrestling men. When they rolled away, I looked desperately for Maria. What I saw sent shocks up my back.

The Dutchman had her pinned to the floor, his saber tip pointed towards her throat. She was resisting him as fiercely and strongly as she could, spitting into his face. He swore and cursed at her. Suddenly, he grunted and his entire body stiffened. Maria had somehow managed to shove her dagger deep in his chest.

"Go to hell," I heard her say in Portuguese. The man didn't respond. He was already dead. She looked disgusted as she pushed the corpse off her body and pulled the dagger out of its chest. There was a deep hole, welling quickly with thick red heart's blood.

By this time, the battle was done. The remaining crew members begged for mercy, only to have Halim slit their throats with his kris. The rest of my men went about the dead bodies, making sure the crew remained dead. The ship was carrying stolen cargo: three bolts of expensive Chinese silk and two large cedar-wood chests. Upon opening the chests, we found eighty gold and silver ingots in each. They must have recently attacked a merchant ship to have such riches. We were in luck. I thanked all the deities, even the saints and bodhisattvas. I had already planned to give some of the gold to Ibu in my next visit to my family home.

Dagger in hand, Maria stood in the sea of corpses, staring numbly at the dead men, including the body of her father's killer.

"It's done," she said in a soft voice. "Rest in peace, Papa and Mama."

She didn't cry. After wiping her dagger clean of blood, she helped the men carry the cargo across the plank, back to our ship.

We left the perahu adrift, the fate of every lanun who died at sea. *Sri Matahari* sailed away, richer and heavier.

۞

"I am voiding our agreement," I told Maria when the ship found shelter at a quiet mangrove swamp. Halim was wading in the soft mud, ready to hunt for the large meaty crabs. We would celebrate later with a meal of boiled mud crab.

"Why? I promised to pay you," Maria sputtered. She seemed to have weathered her first kill well.

"We have two chests of ingots. I am going to give you eight of the gold ones. I hope you can start a new life with them."

"Eight gold ones," Maria let her words trail off.

"We will drop you back in port tomorrow," I said. "Go back to your friend. Pay her one gold ingot as compensation."

"No, I want to stay," Maria said firmly. "I want to stay on the ship. With you."

"I am not your protector."

"You are not," Maria said . "But we swore an oath, remember? *Your life is now mine and my life is now yours.*"

"Ah."

"I want to uphold our oath," she said, watching Halim catch his first mud crab. He was chuckling away like a little boy with his first catch, his face and legs smeared with mud. The men laughed too. It had been a bountiful day.

"I want to travel the Golden Chersonese with the ship . . . with you," she continued, her gaze returning to rest on me. She was very close now. I could smell her. She washed herself thoroughly with our water after the encounter with the lanun. She bore the fragrance of sea salt. Her dagger rested tucked in her belt. "I want to know you better," she said shyly.

My heart rose at those words. I tried to maintain a stern demeanor. "You might get more than what you bargained for."

"The Peranakan matriarch bitch made me do all the menial chores," Maria snorted. "I can endure *anything*."

"Anything? Including me? I can be rather unbearable, just ask Halim." I replied. "Are you sure?"

"You are interesting, Captain Neo," Maria giggled.

"I am only *interesting?*"

Maria laughed her first real laugh. Such a wonderful sound. The men glanced quickly at her, startled by her sudden gaiety.

"Of course," her eyes sparkled merrily. "That is why I want to know you better."

"Indeed," I said. "Indeed."

So, you came into my life like a bodhisattva. We sailed the Golden Chersonese together, you and me, straddlers between the worlds. With two of the gold ingots, I bought you a pair of new boots, no more beaded slippers, but in the latest fashions outside the Golden Chersonese. They were apparently the rage in the courts of the kings and queens. They were made of the finest leather, with the tracery of yellow flower embroidery curling along the edges and the softest of velvet lining their insides. You laughed and said you could run faster with bare feet. "Don't be silly," you said as the sun rose above us in reds and oranges.

I laughed back. You kept the shoes in your private wooden box with the kebaya and sarong. You still wore your silver necklace.

And all was right in the world again.

—fin—

Dear Son

Dear Son,

By the time this letter touches your hands, I am already on my deathbed. Please do not cry for me, for I have lived a long life.

This letter will list down what you have to do after my death. Please follow my instructions. You are my most precious son.

First of all, my books. Give them to schools, to public libraries and to places that need them. Education is important to all. Philosophy is the light of the soul. You should know that, my son.

Secondly, I want you to clean out my cupboards. Give my clothes away to the charities. The underprivileged should have clothes to wear.

Thirdly, make sure my accumulated wealth is shared equally among your ten brothers. My grandchildren will have money to spend.

Now, my son, I want you to read this very carefully as I do not want my body to be cremated or buried.

Donate my organs to Science. I am fairly healthy with no disease or disorder to tarnish or disfigure my vitals. Donate them to Science and research.

My bones should be cleaned and donated to the medical schools. Doctors are our future.

My son, read this carefully now. Amongst my sons, you are the eldest and best and I trust you. You will not fail me in this. Make xiao long bao out of my flesh. Make them small with their tops swirled and perky. Make them filled with hot savory soup.

Mince my flesh with chives and pepper. I want my flesh not too salty. So many people have high blood pressure. There should be a yum cha for my wake. Serve with Pu'Er and Xiang Pian tea. I want to keep on giving, beyond death. I want you to remember me. Please do not question me. Just follow my instructions.

Call Ah Teck. He will know what to do. His name and phone number are attached in a separate piece of paper. Do not lose it.

Please follow my instructions, dear son.

I want you to remember me.

Love,

Your Mother.

—fin—

My Soul Is Wolf

My soul is wolf.

Or that being inside me, in my soul is a wolf or wolf-shaped.

I can see wolf now, dark on dark, shadow on shadow, slinking through forest so layered.

The bells ring, startling me. I awake on my bed, feeling as if I have loped through shrubs, the tunnels made of greenery. My skin smells of sap, mud and dirt. I look at my fingers and am surprised that they are not coated in brown loam.

I hate going to work, dealing with the crowds, listening to the incessant noise humans make. And the smells.

Wolf wants to roll in them, wash the fur thick with them.

Human nose wrinkles, hating everything.

My mind swirls.

With a sigh, I step into class. My students scream my name. That's what my ears perceive.

Wolf retreats and curls up, nose to tail, in a cool dark corner—the Cave.

My soul is wolf.

I have something wolf-shaped, wolf-like, inside.

I don't tell people about wolf. The last time I did, I was sent to a counsellor.

Weekends are the best. I get to run. I get to explore the nearby forest.

I run barefoot, heedless of sharp sticks and stones.

My girlfriend runs with me. I smell her sweat, her hair.

She doesn't yet know about wolf.

My soul is wolf.

Wolf is wolf.

Wolf just is.

Cynthia gifts me a resin replica of a wolf's skull. I don't know how and where she got it. She gives it to me because I love wolves.

"Thank you," I smile. Even smiling feels weird, like I am baring my teeth at her. I should have a wagging tail.

My soul is wolf.

In my dreams, I run naked. No clothes. Nothing. I run naked, and wolf runs besides me, a black shadow. My breasts, my long hair, my skin become nothing.

Then: I become wolf, our bodies and souls intersecting.

My students give me a wolf figurine for Teachers' Day. They shouldn't have. They got the eyes right, those amber staring-at-you eyes.

Wolf stares out of the Cave.

My soul is wolf.

I feel trapped. My surroundings are a concrete zoo. Are there people like me out there?

What should I tell my counsellor?

My parents don't know.

"Your howls sound so real," Dad told me once, when I let loose at night.

Because they are.

"I think I am a wolf," I pluck up enough courage to tell Cynthia.

She stares at me, her mouth idly chewing a piece of chicken. I hear her teeth rubbing against enamel, the moisture between her canines, her tongue moving.

"Like a real wolf?" she asks.

"Maybe. Like it's all inside me," I say.

"Maybe you should start growing fur and teeth during the full moon," she jokes.

I must have reacted, because she begins apologizing profusely. Human expressions are beyond my comprehension.

"I am trying to find out about the fur and teeth bit."

"You are joking, right?"

***

My soul is wolf.

Wolf howls in the forest.

The forest responds with howls.

There are people like me out there.

***

Cynthia tells me she feels like a leopard sometimes. I think she's telling me to comfort me, humor me. She's trying her best. I can't blame her. We are all trying to survive in this hellscape zoo.

She doesn't understand. But she's trying.

***

When the school holidays finally arrive, I book a flight to the nearest forest in a neighboring country. I want to be free. I know they are around. Them. Wolves. Like me. I make contact with a pack online.

We have decided to meet.

Cynthia wants to follow, but I tell her not to.

She's not ready yet.

Even planes scare me, and the wolf within. I tolerate the flight, suppressing the visceral urge to run away.

The taxi brings me to the hotel.

Time to ignore human things.

I find myself standing at the edge of the forest. There is nobody around. No hikers, no tourists. Just the lightening sky and the sigh of the trees.

I strip, and soon I stand nude. Mosquitoes buzz around me.

A howl swells in my throat and fills the air.

I hear howls coming back. They reverberate. The air shivers. My skin shivers.

I begin to stumble at first, and then run run run. The wind in my hair, the wet earth on my paws.

And I never look back.

I will never look back.

Wolf is my soul.

My soul is wolf

—fin—

Treacle Blood

"You don't have to cut open your veins," the old woman warned me, "just to let them feed on you."

It was the day after Qing Ming, when the tombs were swept and the visitors had already left in their cars. The hill of the graves was buried in its usual silence, filled only by the sound of wind and the skitter of spirit voices.

"My blood's treacle," I said quietly to the elder. "Like spun sugar."

"Our lives are not a perpetual Spring Festival," the crone whispered and hobbled down the leaf-covered path, signaling the end of the conversation. She was always like this. I had grown used to her ways. The uncles who swept the tombs and kept the graveyard respected her, often giving her cigarettes and glass bottles she often hung on trees.

With a sigh, I drove off on my moped. I would be back again to seek her healing and counsel.

In the evenings, I sang to the crowd, strumming my guitar to the evening rush-hour traffic. I bared my veins and they fed. I felt good and bad at the same time. Their eyes glistened above their masks, gleaming at the prospect of a good feed.

My blood was treacle. Sweet. They lapped it up like sugar.

"Don't you feel tired after they feed on you?" Anna asked

when I packed up for the night. She had insisted she accompany me when I busked on Singapore's streets.

"Yes," I said and took a sip of the isotonic drink.

"Then why do you keep doing this?" Anna sounded exasperated tonight. It was the full moon. She might turn into her true form later. I kept a close watch on her eyes.

"And this . . . after the virus has ravaged all of us? Why, Dawn, why?" she continued, relentless, like a wolf pursuing her prey.

"You're so pessimistic," I said curtly.

The virus brought change. Even the mildest cases experienced Change. Some grew powerful. Some gained magical strength. Some developed animal traits.

Theories of the virus had percolated, gained popularity and then disappeared as quickly as they appeared. Flu. Cold. Disease. Change. Everyone still wore masks now, afraid of the virus and the change it had brought.

For me, my blood became sweet. Honey. Treacle. And they fed from me even when I bared my soul to the unkind world.

"I don't care if you were a singer or a writer or a poet," Anna growled even as black fur receded back into her skin. I cradled her in my arms. She shivered after her Change, her body trembling from the clash of cells, muscles and transformation.

I kissed her sweaty brow. I didn't care or thought I didn't, because my voice was my life. Wanting to create was my blood. I wanted to sing. I wanted to write.

"They feed from you," Anna said. "I don't like it, Dawn."

"Don't worry. I know how to protect myself," I lied.

※

I remembered watching the spun-sugar artist when he performed his craft in front of admiring eyes. He often showed up, during Spring Festival, at the big fair, spinning molten amber sugar into delicate-looking dragons, phoenixes and gold fish. The air smelled sweet, like burnt sugar. The artist shaped fins, feathers and scales like magic. When I bit into the dragon, sweetness burst in my mouth.

The artist loved making the golden figurines. He also loved the sounds of the admiring crowd.

When I grew up, music and words were my world. I loved making them. And like the spun-sugar artist, I loved the sounds of the crowd.

※

The old woman was at her usual spot amongst the graves of old colonial Singapore. The spirits chattered around her. They smelled me and salivated. She glared at them. Cowed by her stare, they fell back.

"You back for your cleansing ritual, ah?" the elderly lady said. She was the graveyard's guardian. The tomb sweepers gave her a wide berth whenever she was out and about on her business.

I removed my mask. "Yes," I nodded.

"Ah, today you show your true face," she chuckled, amused. "Most of them don't. Do you feel safe around me?"

"I do."

"Strange. The spirits are afraid of me."

"You guard the graves."

"Pity. I'm not usually that frightening."

She lit incense sticks with her beaten-up lighter. The sandalwood smoke wafted over me, creating a thin layer of protection over me. I sighed. I could feel myself healing already.

"So much damage," the old woman tsk-tsked. "They literally gouged you out."

"They were hungry."

"You need to protect yourself more often. Predators will eat and they don't care about your life."

She patched up the holes with the sandalwood smoke and incantations. They only worked for two weeks. Then I would be back again.

While I sat feeling the effects of the smoke infused with my blood, the grave guardian told me stories about Singapore, before the virus came, before Change came. So much joy. So much beauty. But what was normal didn't remain normal. Things went back to normal after that. People still wanted to feed.

What had changed were us. We changed.

I sang once more at the quay where the entertainment thrived and the vampires fed even as they dined on rare steaks and Pinot

Noir. They gave me money. I needed it. They gave me shelter. I loved it.

The one-room apartment I shared with Anna was cosy enough. Having my own piece of air was an illusory joy. Anna made living a thing of beauty. Plants were everywhere in our little home. She placed pots of herbs on the ledge where the sunlight flooded in like a golden sheet. Mint. Rosemary. Lavender. Basil. The air was often fragrant with their sweet and sharp scents. We even salvaged wooden crates from the nearby supermarket for shelves and impromptu tables. We had tea-lights all over the apartment. In the dark, they glowed like tiny suns. This was our home, where we could be normal, relaxed, happy.

When I came back that night, Anna was not home. She had not been home for days now. She now craved being in the open, in the rare forest fragments. I was afraid I had lost her, lost her to the change within her.

Would I be lost too?

Like her?

Suddenly feeling a wave of dizziness, I collapsed on the sofa. The vampires had fed hard tonight. But at least I had money to pay for my rent and bills.

My skin crawled. It felt as if it was inflamed.

I burned. I was on fire.

Then I caught something golden, gleaming down my arm.

Golden liquid flowed down open wounds. I gasped. I was criss-crossed with gold, with amber liquid that smelled like burnt sugar.

"Old lady, can you save them? Please?" the wolf said to the grave guardian. "They are dying."

The grave guardian gazed sadly at the emaciated figure before her. A spider-web of golden streaks covered the skin, dripped down the thighs.

"Aiyah, they are just too far gone," the old lady said, shaking her head. "They should have stopped baring the veins to the jiang shi."

"Is it too late to save them? Please, auntie, please save them."

The grave guardian stared back at the black wolf. A human's eyes gazed back at her.

"I told Dawn to protect themselves. Our lives too fragile to feed a world who wants to eat us."

"And look at them now. So weak, no blood at all."

The old lady lit her incense sticks and readied her incantations.

"I will see what I can do," she declared. The spirits shrank at the tone of her voice.

Then she sang down the skies, the earth and the stars. The sandalwood smoke wrapped the figure like a gentle loving cocoon

And there was silence amongst the graves.

I came to and stared into Anna's golden eyes.

You need to stop feeding them, the wolf seemed to plead.

Please stop, I beg you.

I sang to the crowd.

I needed to.
My golden blood flowed inside me, singing, dancing, glowing.
I sang.
They fed.
The wounds grew bigger.

I beg you.
Please stop.

I sang.

The old woman shook her head.
"The sandalwood smoke can't protect you forever."

I sang because I had treacle blood.
I would keep on baring my veins to them.
I didn't know why.

Please stop.

When I visited the graveyard, the old crone was no longer there. The uncles told me that she was "just gone" like that. Like incense smoke. She left me a present, apparently. They came back with bundle of sandalwood incense sticks.

In the wind, I heard her gentle laughter.

—fin—

The Year Is 2115

It is the year 2115.

I know it sounds all high and mighty, victorious and grand. But we have made it, haven't we? 2115. People thought we would never survive it, let alone thrive in this world. Ma and Papa are relieved. We survived right? A deadly pandemic. The ice caps melting. Civil wars. Countries cutting ties and retreating into their own walled borders. The historians call it *Apocalypse*. End of the world. Yet, here I stand, beside the window of my small apartment flat, staring out into the glittering bay area with its shining buildings, conservatories and Giant Trees that absorb light and water. Already this early in the morning, small boats are speeding across the water. Their wakes trail white curves on the surface. The silver delivery drones are whizzing about with their precious cargo of letters and parcels. Everything feels good. Normal.

Nothing seems to have changed.

The sky is a watery reflection, made blurry by the sizzling shield that covers the city like a glass globe. I can't see much beyond the sizzle, beyond its edge.

It is the year 2115.

Milestone!

New year, new beginnings!

I know, I know. I will the timer to stop ringing, because I have to work. Plants do not water themselves nor feed themselves organic fertilisers. No, what New Year resolution did I make a few hours earlier? Something about harvesting the best bok choy the whole of SEA has seen. I made a bet with my supervisor, a bet which I will probably lose. I tend to break New Year resolutions all the time.

My neighbours wave at me as they spray water on their own container plants. Our founder would be so proud. Temasek has truly become a Garden City. Suddenly many people want to be gardeners. Horticulture is the hot subject every student wants to take. Believe me, I am a certified gardener, at one of the biggest skyscraper farms, growing the best produce in the region and winning prizes everywhere. Best of all, people are sharing their produce with one another.

We are all happy gardeners.

Yet, as much as the Garden City is also now a Science Fiction city, old comforts still exist. I pass by the old uncle selling you tiao and soy bean milk served hot in recyclable paper cups. I buy some and thank him. He tells me stories about Temasek in the past, 50 years ago.

"Used to be more exciting, you know," the old uncle will tell me. It is often a repetition of a previous story. "More stalls selling things you will never eat now. Wet markets, you know. Chicken in cages."

"Chicken in cages?" I gasp, appalled.

"Ah, yes. And rabbits too."

I think he is pulling my leg. But he looks oddly sincere, even wistful. Uncle must be in his late 70s.

"Let me tell you about the last blackout we had . . ."

I smile politely and leave quickly before he launches into a soliloquy.

Then, I stride past the bird song admirers who pamper their birds as much as I pamper my plants. All these birds are regulated. Poaching is now a major crime, to the relief of the animal protection groups and supporters of animal welfare. Some of the farms I know breed songbirds, their genetic lineages kept under lock and key by the conservatories. Posters with graphics are plastered all over the wall, warning of dire consequences. The birds are protected. So many species have died.

Boarding the maglev train, I look out beyond the bay, beyond the sizzle of the shield that protects Temasek from the outside world. From everything else. It's been there as long as I could remember. It's like it's part of ancient history, but not really. Ma and Papa talk about it all the time. The Globe keeps things out.

The you tiao is hot in my hands. I will savour it in my office. My SMART chirps. My friends are now online. We are all connected.

Supervisor

It is the year 2115.

I tell myself this when I walk down the rows of gleaming green vegetables, my sensor wand testing the temperature level. It beeps NORMAL. I smile, satisfied.

Rows 14, 15 and 16 are due for harvesting. I make a note so that my young assistant will do so in the next 24 hours. She is munching away at her you tiao—*fried dough fritters! how quaint!*—in her little cubicle. How pleasurable, being single and young and care-free.

I know that my eyes have bags and I look like the

third-generation pandas in the zoological gardens. "I probably look cute," I told my partner this morning, and she glared at me. Our baby wakes us up for his nightly feeds. He is such a fussy baby. So far, she has been bearing the brunt of breastfeeding and diapering him. I try to help. But I am not a good mother ... I can't even change a diaper correctly! Baby coos and giggles at my partner who cuddles him. Me? I feel like a brick.

My sensor wand suddenly buzzes. Heat discrepancy in rows 19 and 20. Annoying. The solar panels need maintenance.

"Is the Globe on the fritz?" I question my assistant when I shrug off my suit and gloves.

"It looked fine when I was on board the train," she says. Her SMART data pad glows open before her. I pretend not to see that she is playing the latest cat collecting game. A plump tabby is playing with a ball of pink yarn. I also see that she is on the WEAVE, chatting with her friends. Chat boxes are blinking in and out. The WEAVE is a huge part of people's lives here, a social network of friends, colleagues and families. Our little bubble. I wonder if I should re-activate my account ... Have been so busy, of late.

Wasn't there something similar in the past? I am not sure. Many things became obsolete, didn't they?

I am going to question HQ. They should know.

It is the year 2115. We figured everything out, didn't we?

I think about my partner and my son. Our home needs more energy. Laundry, food, the ever-growing pile of dishes ...

The Globe can't keep everything out, right?

We survived everything. 2115. A milestone. We can survive this.

Whatever this is.

Oh yes, the solar panels ...

Assistant

"It is the year 2115," some chirpy DJ states and asks his listeners for opinions. Most of them are inane and I laugh at most of them. "People thought we wouldn't make it but we did!" "We are a nation young and free! Not anymore! Haha!" I blow raspberries at the radio, a retro unit I managed to take from Papa who is pretty protective over his collections. He has everything, including books on zoology and botany. I turn my attention to the stir-fry, some of the kai lan and Chinese kale from row 11. I toss in some strips of chicken. It is touted to be Kampung Chicken, because the fowl run free in the farms. The you tiao uncle talked about caged chicken . . . Imagine that.

Either way, it is going to be my delicious dinner. I scroll through the WEAVE, giggling at my friends making fun of the radio show.

The light flickers and I look up, halfway picking a strip of chicken with my chopsticks. I hear some people yelling down the corridor. Another flicker—and then, the room is just dark. The hum of appliances and devices goes dead. The air is suddenly very still.

"What the fu . . ." I mutter. A blackout is rare. I fumble in the dark to the window. There is a lot of shouting, people like me, fumbling in the dark. The entire area is plunged into darkness. I see . . . stars. I shouldn't be seeing stars. Stars are . . .

The Globe is down.

Didn't the you tiao uncle say something about a blackout . . . ?

But that was a long time ago . . .
The Globe is down.
The shield is down.
Why is it down?
Is it supposed to be down?

Supervisor

It is the year 2115!

Somewhere in the apartment, I hear baby wailing his head off and my partner trying to comfort him. I curse at the lack of candles. Must always keep spares! I hear my mom in my head. She always reminds me. She remembers other times.

I stare out of the window. Normally, we still get moonlight, even with the Globe. I see a white crescent, like a cut finger nail, in the sky.

A sensation like cold water trickling down my back makes me start. I realize I am afraid. The Globe is down.

The Globe is down.

A matchstick hisses in the dark and there is a soft glow, illuminating my partner's worried face.

We hear the chop chop chop of helicopters. The roof rumbles at their passing.

I lean over and give my son a gentle kiss on the forehead. That's all I can give to him. Our son. I want to protect him.

We will survive this.

Assistant

It turns out that a flock of Javan mynahs has hit the main solar power generator linked to the Giant Trees, causing the Globe to short out. The news is full of people commiserating, people helping each other on the WEAVE, and scenes of candlelight and laughter. Everyone is treating it as a joke, as something to remember for a long time, but something also inconsequential. The WEAVE calls it the Problem.

"It will not happen again," the old you tiao seller tells me sagely. "They will fix the problem. They always do."

"Will they, uncle?" I ask half-incredulously, half-believing.

His wrinkled face bears a wide smile. "Yeah, lah, they will fix the problem. Our gahmen will. They always do. See, we are using sunlight as energy! They will surely think of something."

Gahmen. That's one old word they use to describe our government. Papa uses it too. In a joking manner.

With the Globe down, strange things are happening.

Flocks of birds flow in, as if the air currents have brought them. Wild birds!

Odd smells linger in the air—petroleum, sea water, and loam. Like the deepest brownest of soil.

"But it is the year 2115!" I argue with Papa over the telephone. My family is worried enough to have a face-to-face conference with me onscreen. I see Papa's lined face, his shaking head, and Ma at the background, making comments about the Globe and Taiwanese media making fun of our Problem. "I thought things were going to change for the better! We can't keep everything out."

Papa snorts. "Well, things happen. Not everything is perfect. You know, when Temasek was a sleepy fishing village . . ."

"Aw, Pa. Not this again!" I almost shout. Something straight out of my history textbook, something . . . boring? Can it explain the Problem away?

"You know, they say that they are going to take a week to fix it," Ma interjects, barging into the conversation. "A week!"

"They still need to find the parts mah," Pa replies idly. "I heard they still manufacture the parts in China."

I let my parents argue over the Globe and the Problem it has become.

Something flitters into my room. It is a bright blue butterfly.

I catch it in an empty glass bottom. The butterfly shimmers with its own light. I am mesmerised by it. My WEAVE buzzes. They are talking about having a party at the Edge of the Globe on Saturday. Two days later.

I decide to take the butterfly with me to the party, if it can live that long. *What should I feed it with?*

Supervisor

The plants in the farms are reacting strangely now. No matter how indoors and up high in the air, they are responding to something. The kai lan flowers. The bok choy grows bigger and bigger. So much for New Year resolutions. I lost my bet with my assistant . She was so happy that she won. Meanwhile, the smell of the earth grows stronger and stronger. Are the bok choy reacting to fresh natural air? It is the year 2115 and we are acting like curious children. People are starting to flock towards the edge of the Globe, where our borders reach the sea. Ah, the

Globe. It keeps everything out. People are looking out now, pointing at the derelict container ships and the debris left over from the Apocalypse. The sea levels rose, didn't they? Now the shield is down. We can approach the outside world as if it were a wild animal.

We have become tourists in our own country.

"Monitor rows 30, 31 and 32," I say sternly to my assistant, who looks as if she has not slept. She yawns and nods. I notice she has something fluttering in a clear glass bottle on her desk. It is a butterfly with the brightest bluest wings I have ever seen. Its wings shimmer. The only time I have seen one was when I was a little girl, at my Gong Gong's garden. It danced around me in circles.

My partner wants to visit the Edge of the Globe, as people have termed it. "Come on, where's your sense of adventure?" she challenges me, with a teasing smile and laughing eyes.

"Sense of adventure? I have thrown it away," I retort back.

"Oh, come on," my partner nudges me. "I will make spaghetti!"

"Why do they call it 'Edge of the Globe'?"

"Something's happening at the edge? I don't know. The WEAVE comes up with weird terms all the time."

I bite my lower lip. "It's a big party, apparently. C'mon, it will be fun!" my partner nudges me harder. "Don't be such a wet blanket."

I hesitate, staring at her and our baby. Perhaps, I should make my way to the edge. See what the fuss is about.

Assistant

"It is the year 2115!" a girl gushes as she poses for her SMART drone as it hovers in front of her. "Smile!" Her pictures and words go straight to the WEAVE. I hear the pings as people signal their likes and favorites about her self-blog. Self-blogs are very popular, often detailing the lives of WEAVE users.

The Edge of the Globe is close now. I make my way carefully. There is mud. Close to me, people throng the narrow pathway. They are all laughing and cheerful.

I can smell the sea now. It is so strong that my nose wrinkles. I hold onto the glass bottle in my hands. My supervisor thinks I have gone slightly crazy, carrying this butterfly around. I think she's stressed with work and her son.

I feel sorry for her.

Something huge rears up in front of me. I pause, look up and stare. It is all corroding metal and dangling steel cables. The metal groans and moans with the wind. The thing rises before me like a cliff. Flocks of sea birds are spiraling around it. Many have made nests in its cracks and holes.

A long time ago, it was a container ship.

I stare at it. My eyes begin to water. It is a stark reminder of our own mortality. So many people had died. Competition. Throwing vulnerable people under. Then a raging disease. Shipping crashed literally. *Apocalypse.*

Was life that different before everything died? Before the Globe was built? Were people that greedy? That ... *bad*?

Fortunately, we don't live like that anymore. We shouldn't live like that. But are we kinder now? Do the container vegetables we are growing at home and in our skyscraper farms teach us about helping one another? Are we? Self-reliance and resilience are all over in our textbooks, in our media, like they are the best values ever.

Are we only helping ourselves?

While people take pictures of the hulk, I cry at its passing.

When my tears are dry, I unstop the glass bottle. The blue butterfly perches at the mouth, as if it is thinking of freedom. It has lived that long enough.

"Go, you silly!" my voice croaks.

The butterfly takes a tentative step out. Another, several wing flaps, and it lifts off. I watch it disappear into the distance, where the dancing birds are.

۞

Supervisor

"Watch your step," I warn my partner as we make our way down the pathway. Our son is snug in his baby sling. We see many couples with their children. My heart grows warm.

My assistant passes me by, looking as if she has been crying. I wave to her and she smiles back before walking quickly towards the maglev line. She's carrying an empty glass bottle. It is the same I'd seen on her desk.

The hulk is there, an ancient relic from the past. We both stare up, up, up at it, inhaling its scent of decay, history and something else. There are birds nesting in there. The noise of their songs echoes in the cavern in the hull.

"It is the year 2115," I say softly and hold my partner's hand. "It's a milestone. We made it. So many things have changed. Some for the better, some not so. Temasek survived through all this. We will live."

My partner leans against me for a brief moment, before our son stirs and begins fretting. He lets me carry him. His cries mingle with the sounds of the sea-birds. Terns, I realize, they are terns. The scientist in me wants to jot down the observation, inform HQ and then do what . . . ? Write a paper about the return of terns? Petition to have the old species recorded?

I marvel at the terns' beauty. This will suffice. Things are fleeting. Transient. Even peace and happiness. Better to cherish them now.

"They say the Globe will be up by midnight," my partner checks her SMART. "Let's enjoy this scene while it lasts."

All things are transient.

Groups of people troop past us. They are carrying bunches of candles in baskets. Teenagers give us two white ones. We settle down with the rest, staring at the stars as they slowly come out in the night sky. We share our pasta with others in a communal picnic. As the lights begin to fade, lit candles shimmer into existence, like stars in the night. Shimmer, shimmer.

—fin—

Solarpunk Letters: Seeds of Change

What is joy but the morning sun glowing on to the fruits you have grown. What is pleasure but the sweet honey of its juice going down your throat.
*

The people join hands in celebration. The planting is done. As they mingle, windmills turn wind into energy. It is a gentle hum, like a heartbeat, in the earth-tone houses.
*

Leaves glisten, the dew like miniature pearls. Vertical rows of bak choy, tomatoes and kale. Seedlings remain protected in their tiny sun rooms.
*

The carp dance in the water. They are moving Chinese calligraphy, watercolour painting turning into life. Above them the lotuses open to the sun and the huge circular leaves act as shade.
*

They manage to fix the panels. There is a sign of relief from all the groups. The sound of children playing is joyous music.
*

What is joy but the sound of crisp clean wind in your hair. What is pleasure but the feel of water on your skin.
*

Individuals pair up or move in trios. Family. Friends. Lovers. Diverse. Above them the tree takes in light and gives out oxygen.

*

During festival time, the children hang letters they rolled up tight and inserted into old glass bottles on trellises. Wishes for the future. Encouragement for people they care about. The bottles will be recycled. The trellises kept for the next festival. People take a bottle and read the letter within.

*

The forests are safe. Every weekend the children come and learn the ways of the trees, the animals and the insects.

*

What is hope but a green seedling cupped in your hands. What is hope but a letter to the future.

—fin—

Rose Jam: A Pandemic Recipe

Rose Jam

(A Pandemic Recipe)

Feeds four.

(With anything in sight—bread, cheese, essentials)

Ingredients

- Roses.

(I bought these from a supermarket, but I know some of you can get it online—lucky you!—and some of you grow roses. Of course, I washed my hands with hot water and soap the moment I got back and showered too. My skin is so dry from the constant washing. Oh yeah, wear a mask when you are out)

- White cane sugar, three full tablespoons.

(Sugar is an essential, apparently, together with baking flour and yeast. The shelves are empty, you damn panic-buyers and hoarders! If not, use honey, but honey is also sold out)

- Pectin.

(I don't know how you are going to get pectin, so this jam will be the most basic, don't complain)

- Lemon zest

(The lemons are gone from the fresh produce section)

- Chilli flakes (optional).

(Chilli flakes also sold out)

- A sterilised jam jar.

(I used an old jar. The crowds who packed IKEA cleaned out the rest of the jam jars and containers, but I hear they started a new cluster of infections)

Method

- Wash your hands with soap.
- Get a clean stainless steel pot.
- Wash the roses thoroughly with water and then pluck off the petals.
- Wash your hands.
- Fill the stainless steel pot with clean water, add the petals and sugar in. Stir until the solution boils. Lower the heat.
- Make sure the petals soften and the colour of the solution changes. Depends on the colour of the roses.
- Wash your hands.
- When the solution is more or less thick, let it cool and then pour it into the sterilised jam jar.
- Wash your hands again.

(You can eat it with bread, cheese, anything you can find in your kitchen. Or straight from it and savour it while imagining you are in a garden brimming with flowers, the sunlight warm and golden on your skin)

(If you are of the social justice sort, make jam for your neighbours because they will appreciate small things during this time. For fuck's sake, don't turn into one of those awful snitches who complain much about people leaving their houses. Make jam, make something, for the people around you instead!

Don't be selfish and panic-buy!

Fight capitalism from ground up. This is the time when women's work, unpaid labour, is actually feeding, nourishing and keeping the community going. Capitalism can go fuck itself!

Plus jam-making is such a privilege, isn't it? Even buying roses is a privilege.

And remember to wash your hands frequently and stay indoors!)

—fin—

Working From Home

I have been a school girl studying for her matriculation exams. I have been a suburban mom with three kids, one with special needs. I have been a Kpop fan. I have been a farmer angry with the government. I have been a gay man who supports his presidential candidate. I have been a furious woman who wants to protect her bodily autonomy.

I get paid for being all these people. I have three phones, one for each job. My mom thinks I work from home, which is not far from the truth. My employers send me gigs. It's the gig economy, why not? My girl goes to school. My mom gets her medication.

One day, it would be social media posts about certain issues.

Another day, it would be social media posts about certain people.

I sometimes jump in and make people angry. I used to get upset seeing people angry over . . . lies. But I soon grew a thicker skin. It's just a job, you see. A job. I log in from 9 in the morning and log out around 5pm. In between I have sent out about 200 social media posts. My accounts are all popular. I have huge followings. They all think I am real. Of course, I am real.

Early morning. I wake up at the sound of the ringing alarm bell from my tablet. I get up as well, wake my youngest up.

I join other moms at the school gate, laughing, joking.

Katie wants to get her hair done today. I tell her to wait, because her exams are coming.

I send Thomas to the speech therapist. He's slowly improving, Michelle promises me. He's learning how to make eye contact now, though he still has mini meltdowns in the middle of the mall. Noises scare him. He wants his socks arranged in a particular way.

Dinner has to be planned carefully. Thomas doesn't like peas. Loves peanut butter.

The dreams have gotten weird. They have gotten real. Too real.

I wake up, holding empty air. In the dream, I am holding a fork. We were having dinner.

Nevermind. I get back to work.

Today, it's all talking about vaccinations. My suburb mom tweets about protecting her family's interests, especially her son's. She is vaccine-shy, she tweets. The retweets multiply, the likes soar. I ignore the angry replies.

I kiss Emil passionately on the lips. We have tied the knot!

Around us, our friends cheer, waving the rainbow flags.

We have so many plans in mind. But I want Emil to be well first.

We run to the waiting limo as flower petals drift down like a blizzard.

Sex is hot. I think we woke the neighbours up.

Too real, too real.

I am working too hard. I text my employer that I need a short break. He tells me that they are very close to winning the election. Just one more week, he says.

I get paid in various currencies, which I change at the money changer. Together, I earn up to 3000 each month. Enough to cover schools, medications, groceries. Nobody asks me what I actually do.

Work from home, I say. Half-true, half-lie.

Meanwhile, my accounts post whatever they are tasked to post. The retweets explode. I think I am beginning to get addicted to the likes. My adrenaline surges at the sound of the notifications pinging. Pinging pinging pinging. Pure euphoria.

SOON will be starting their world tour! I have posters of them all over my wall. They are all so cute. The last time they visited, we all camped overnight at the airport. When they came out from the departure gate, the screaming was huge.

Park Bin is so handsome. He's my favourite. I have a body pillow with his likeness on it.

I write fic and post on a fanfiction site. I get kudos all the time.

"What exactly are you doing?" Mom asks me one day. Her gentle lined face hovers in front of me. I am in the middle of typing a long post, one that would drive engagement off the charts. This gig will earn me a month's worth of rent, medication and groceries.

"I am busy, ma," I say.

"Tsk tsk," she replies. "You never tell me what you do."

"I work from home and you get your medication," I snap. My tone is too harsh. I instantly regret it. Mom backs off and doesn't talk to me for the whole night.

Feeling bad, I make her mung bean soup.

Then, I read to my girl. I bought a new picture book with my last salary. I wasn't able to afford one the last time.

My crops are all dying. Too much and they rot in the sun. What's the government doing? Nothing! Meanwhile, my family starves, my crops die.

I am angry, of course! Why shouldn't I be?

People go hungry and I see my friends pouring milk away. Milk that could have fed so many thousands!

I hold my youngest grandson in my arms. He waves his chubby hands at him. Everything melts away. I want him to have a future.

I ignore the dreams. One day before the election. And then, I get paid. It will be more than I'd usually earn. 5000.

So, I am that person on social media with the axe to grind, the agenda to push, the outrage to fan. I make people angry. As they say, haters gonna hate. It's my job.

They don't care if I am real or not. Most of my followers think I am. The school girl. The suburban mom. The gay man who supports a presidential candidate. The angry farmer. People become attached to my posts, wait for my updates, and pour emotional replies all over me. My fake lives captivate them. They give advice, support and encouragement. They hang onto my every word. They love drama and I give them what they want.

⁂

"Hey, you," a voice wakes me from my reverie. I start, turn around, and see a young teenage girl standing in the middle of the kitchen. It's the day of the election. I am tired, but I am close to earning out my gig for this month. 5000. That's a lot of money.

The teenager isn't my daughter. She shouldn't be back from school this early. The teenager is wearing a uniform I can't recognise. A blue pinafore, white blouse. A neat ponytail. Singapore? I don't know. I am hazy when it comes to school uniforms.

"Hey, you," she says. She's carrying a bag with badges on them. Kpop badges. SOON.

Oh no.

I open my mouth and nothing comes out.

"Yes, you," another voice, a male one, joins her. Movement at the corner of my eye. Then, a man, in his thirties, appears. He's wearing a grey turtle-neck and faded jeans. On the lapel of his collar is a small rainbow flag. On the other side of the collar is an . . . AIDS AWARE badge.

A grizzled old gentleman in dirty dungarees and rubber boots hobbles forward. He smells of the earth and something else: rotting vegetation. *Rotting, because it had been out too long in the sun. Unharvested.*

"You," he rasps.

I gasp, but I am paralysed. I try to reach for my phone, my own personal phone. I want to call my mom. The teenage girl knocks it away from my hand.

"You pretend to be us," she says. "Stop being us. Stop using our identities."

"You are not real," I manage to bite out.

"Somewhere out there, there are people like us," the gay man says. "We are real."

"Stop using our identities," the farmer grouses and bangs the kitchen table loudly. "Stop being us."

"You. Are. Not. Real."

I want to scream. Shout.

They are not real, right? I made them up. I . . . made them up.

Without warning, the three figures walk towards me.

"Stop. What are you doing?!"

Without speaking a word, they seem to melt into me. I see the Kpop badges swirling before me, the dungarees crawling up my legs, the face of the teenage girl seeping into my chest. It's agony, it's like slipping into ice-cold water.

"Ma!" My daughter's voice, this time. Real. Her voice is real. "What's wrong? Did you faint?"

I open my eyes to see her leaning over me, shaking my shoulders.

The teenager, the gay man and the old farmer are gone.

I get paid. I see the amount in my bank account. For a brief moment, I am happy. But what's happiness anyway?

I remove the sim cards and delete everything off the phones. I throw two out into the bin. I still have to keep one. For communication's sake, I tell myself.

I apply for a proper writing job.

"What's your job about?" My mom asks.

"I write," I say.

"Work from home?" She has a twinkle in her eye, a half-smile on her lips.

"Yes, but it will be about fashion," I say. I stare at my mass communications diploma. Maybe it's time I use it for good.

You are us.

You are us.

You are us.

—fin—

Wives At The End Of The World

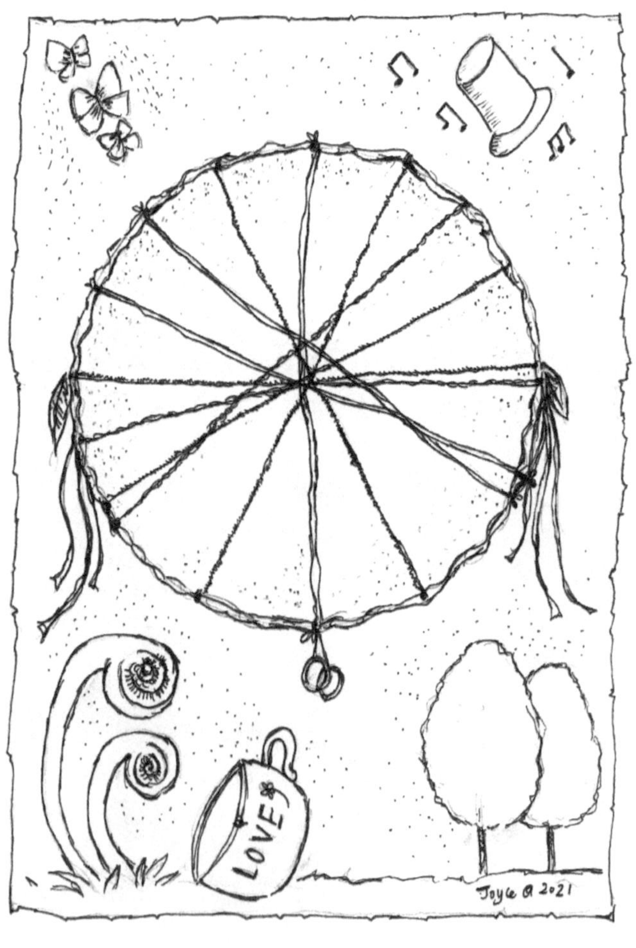

Solidarity

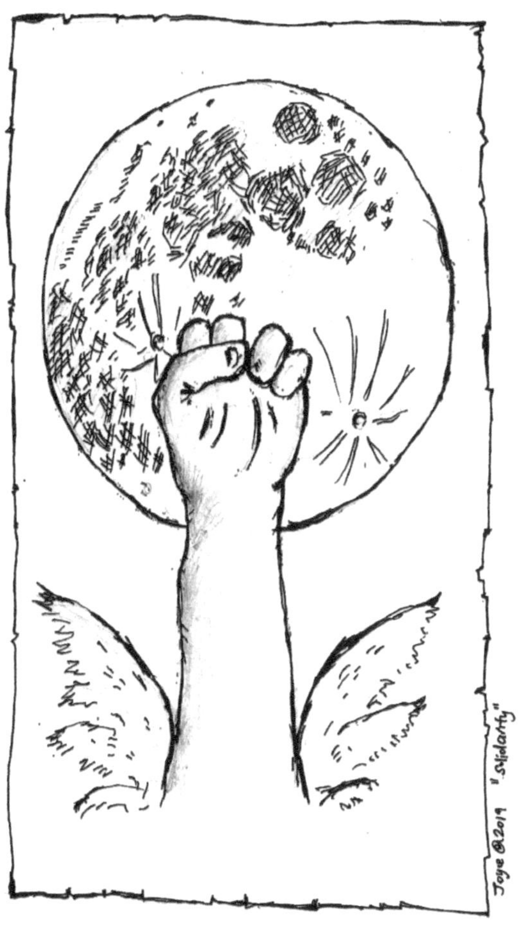

Conclusion

There you have it: New Trails, Terrain, and The Land.

I realize that the landscape might be incomplete or missing in detail. Indeed I have omitted the series (both science fiction, young adult and middle grade) I have written as well as picture books. Not to mention the sf-nal nonfiction editorial work and games/ttrpg writing I have done. Sometimes people might think I have spread myself too thin, but the landscape is my own and mine to explore. A wolf can and will carve out its territory.

And it is my milestone. Half a century of exploring, of existing, of living. It has been so hard at times, so painful. I also realize that many of the stories are in first-person; perhaps, I wrote them in this way because I *felt* so intensely, so personally. The stories are the result of my own internal navigations, myself dealing with pain. In these past seventeen, almost twenty, years, pain has been my constant companion. But . . . I hasten to add: there is also joy too. I need to remember the joy.

Write. No Excuses.

Write.
I can't.
Write.
I hurt.
Write.
I say 'no' and linger longer.
Write, write, write.

Write, you fool.
I can't, I can't.
My body hurts.
My soul hurts.
My energy is gone.
Write, you idiot.
It doesn't matter.
You still need to speak,
Need to get that thing out of you.
Write. No excuses.

⁂

More to years of exploring and of nurturing the path. More to
joy and experiencing.

⁂

The earth waits for the rain to come.
The seeds wait for the blessed kiss of moisture
To anoint them, to germinate—
Wait, wait, wait.
Be patient.
Wait.

Wait.
Be patient.
Wait, wait, wait.
The seeds will germinate—

The seeds will wait for the moisture to kiss them.
The earth will continue to persist.

Acknowledgements

A wolf is the most strongest with its pack around it.

I am immensely grateful to Emily of Atthis Arts for giving the collection a home and a place.

I am also grateful to Patricia E. Matson for her proofreading. It takes a collective and a village to make a book. Thank you to Dhiyanah, Stewart, and Alex for the extra eyes!

I am in debt to Jaymee Goh for their friendship. Steampunk Southeast Asia for the win! We will create our own Steampunk Nusantara one day.

I am in awe of Judith Tarr, mentor and great supporter. Your books inspired me and continue to persist on, like a bright fire in my heart.

Lastly, I am thankful for my family for being there for and with me. And to all who have supported and lifted me for all these years: a big Thank You from my heart.

About the Author

Joyce Chng lives in Singapore. Their speculative fiction has appeared in *The Apex Book of World SF II*, *We See A Different Frontier*, *Cranky Ladies of History*, and *Accessing The Future*. Joyce also co-edited *THE SEA IS OURS: Tales of Steampunk Southeast Asia* with Jaymee Goh. Their novels span across wolf clans (*Starfang: Rise of the Clan*), vineyards (*Water into Wine*) and swordmaking forges (*Fire Heart*) respectively. Joyce also wrangles article editing at Strange Horizons. Alter-ego J. Damask writes about werewolves in Singapore. *Star Pattern Traveller*, a novella about first contact, was published in February 2024.

You can find Joyce at

awolfstale.wordpress.com

@jolantru.bsky.social on Bluesky

(Pronouns: she/her, they/their)

About the Artist

Mr. Amorn Setthitorn is an artist working in folk and primitive techniques from Chiang Mai Thailand. His work seeks to learn from nature and reveal the emotional, spiritual, and way of life from times where man and nature were living close together. In Buddhism, the philosophy of "our life exists through involvement with others" explains this relationship. Whenever we destroy our surroundings, we are destroying ourselves as well.

"A Matter of Possession" originally published in *Crossed Genres Magazine*, 2009.

"Growing Up" originally published in *Crossed Genres Magazine*, 2009.

"A Basketful of Figs" originally published on Wattpad, 2013.

"The Sound of Breaking Glass" originally published in *Semaphore Magazine* 2010, also published in the *Semaphore Anthology 2010*, edited by Marie Hodgkinson, and the *Apex Book of World SF, Volume 2*, edited by Lavie Tidhar, Apex Book Company, 2011.

"The Bones Shine Through With Light" originally published in *M-BRANE-SF* Issue 27, 2011, also published in *Insignia Vol. 1: Japanese Fantasy Stories*, edited by Kelly Matsuura, 2013, *Unconventional Fantasy: A Celebration of Forty Years of the World Fantasy Convention*, edited by Bill Campbell, Sam Lubell, Peggy Raw Sapienz, and Jean Marie Ward, 2014, and *Sunspot Jungle Vol. 1* edited by Bill Campbell, Rosarium Publishing, 2018.

"Yao Jin" originally published in *Weird Noir*, edited by Kate Laity, Fox Spirit Books, 2012.

"Lotus" originally published in *We See a Different Frontier: A postcolonial speculative fiction anthology*, edited by Fabio Fernandes and Djibril al-Ayad, Futurefire.net Publishing, 2013.

"A Sky Full of Swiftlets" originally published in *Visibility Fiction*, 2013.

"The Lessons of the Moon" originally published in *Accessing The Future*, edited by Kathryn Allan and Djibril al-Ayad, Futurefire.net Publishing, 2015.

"Being Invisible" originally published in *Uncanny Magazine*, 2018.

"I Found Love In An Urn Full of Ashes" originally published in *Insignia Vol. 4: Asian Fantasy Stories*, edited by Kelly Matsuura, 2017.

"Diary of War" originally published in *Anathema Magazine*, 2017.

"Silver Wings" originally published in *The Future Fire*, 2019.

"Garra Rufa" originally published in *Rambutan Literary*, 2017.

"Qi Xi" originally published in *Uncanny Magazine*, 2017.

"The Bridge" originally published in *Anathema Magazine*, 2018.

"Saints And Bodhisattvas" originally published in *Scourge of the Seas of Time (and Space)*, edited by Catherine Lundoff, Queen of Swords Press, 2018, and also published in *BE: ME: LGBTQIA+ Stories of Belong*, edited by Joel Donato Ching Jacob and Daphne Lee, ASEAN SOGIE Caucus, 2021.

"Dear Son" originally published in The Sharp & Sugar Tooth, edited by Octavia Cade, Upper Rubber Boot Books, 2019.

"My Soul Is Wolf" originally published in *Anathema Magazine*, 2020.

"Treacle Blood" originally published in *The Future Fire*, 2022.

"It Is the Year 2115" originally published in *Multispecies Cities: Solarpunk Urban Futures*, edited by C. Rupprecht, D. Cleland, N. Tamura, R. Chaudhuri, and S. Ulibarri, World Weaver Press, 2021.

"Solarpunk Letters: Seeds of Change" originally published in *The Future Fire*, 2023.

"Rose Jam: A Pandemic Recipe" originally published in *Wolf's Path*, 2025.

"Working From Home" originally published in *Wolf's Path*, 2025.

"Wives At The End of The World" originally published in *The Future Fire*, 2021.

"Solidarity" originally published in *The Future Fire*, 2019.